BRADNER LIBRARY
SCHOOLCRAFT COLLEGE
LIVONIA, MICHIGAN 48152

RB 140 .G762 2011

Growth disorders

WITHDRAWN

DATE DUE

1st EDITION

Perspectives on Diseases and Disorders

Growth Disorders

Mary E. Williams
Book Editor

Detroit • New York • San Francisco • New Haven, Conn • Waterville, Maine • London

Elizabeth Des Chenes, *Managing Editor*

© 2012 Greenhaven Press, a part of Gale, Cengage Learning

Gale and Greenhaven Press are registered trademarks used herein under license.

For more information, contact:
Greenhaven Press
27500 Drake Rd.
Farmington Hills, MI 48331-3535
Or you can visit our Internet site at gale.cengage.com

ALL RIGHTS RESERVED.
No part of this work covered by the copyright herein may be reproduced, transmitted, stored, or used in any form or by any means graphic, electronic, or mechanical, including but not limited to photocopying, recording, scanning, digitizing, taping, Web distribution, information networks, or information storage and retrieval systems, except as permitted under Section 107 or 108 of the 1976 United States Copyright Act, without the prior written permission of the publisher.

For product information and technology assistance, contact us at

Gale Customer Support, 1-800-877-4253
For permission to use material from this text or product, submit all requests online at www.cengage.com/permissions

Further permissions questions can be emailed to permissionrequest@cengage.com

Articles in Greenhaven Press anthologies are often edited for length to meet page requirements. In addition, original titles of these works are changed to clearly present the main thesis and to explicitly indicate the author's opinion. Every effort is made to ensure that Greenhaven Press accurately reflects the original intent of the authors. Every effort has been made to trace the owners of copyrighted material.

Cover image © Lester V. Bergman/Corbis

LIBRARY OF CONGRESS CATALOGING-IN-PUBLICATION DATA

Growth disorders / Mary E. Williams, book editor.
    p. cm. -- (Perspectives on diseases and disorders)
 Summary: "Growth Disorders: Understanding Growth Disorders; Issues and Controversies Surrounding Growth Disorders; Living with Growth Disorders"--Provided by publisher.
 Includes bibliographical references and index.
 ISBN 978-0-7377-5774-3 (hardback)
 1. Growth disorders--Popular works. I. Williams, Mary E., 1960-
    RB140.G763 2011
    616.4'7--dc23
                                                            2011028582

Printed in the United States of America
1 2 3 4 5 6 7 15 14 13 12 11

CONTENTS

Foreword   8

Introduction   10

CHAPTER 1   Understanding Growth Disorders

1. Growth Disorders: An Overview   16
   Neil Izenberg and Steven A. Dowshen
   Growth disorders may be caused by poor nutrition, abnormal hormonal levels, genetic mutations, atypical bone-growth conditions, tumors, and other diseases.

2. Achondroplasia: A Common Form of Dwarfism   27
   Rebecca J. Frey
   Short-limb dwarfism, a genetic mutation that affects bone development, is the most common form of abnormally short stature in adults.

3. Excessive Growth Hormone Leads to Gigantism and Acromegaly   33
   National Endocrine and Metabolic Disease Information Service
   Acromegaly and gigantism are usually the result of tumors that cause the pituitary gland to produce excessive amounts of growth hormone. In children, symptoms include sudden and marked growth. Adulthood symptoms include joint aches, sleep apnea, weakness, and thickened skin.

4. Diagnosing and Treating Marfan Syndrome 45
   March of Dimes Foundation
   People with Marfan syndrome often have unusually long arms, legs, and fingers. The disorder varies in severity and may include other health challenges such as scoliosis, glaucoma, and heart valve abnormalities.

5. Turner Syndrome: A Chromosomal Deficit Exclusive to Girls 56
   Turner Syndrome Society of the United States
   One cause of short stature in girls is Turner syndrome, a chromosomal disorder that also leads to early ovarian failure and incomplete puberty.

6. The Use and Abuse of Human Growth Hormone 62
   The Hormone Foundation
   Synthetic growth hormone is safe and effective when prescribed for certain conditions, but abusing it can lead to dangerous side effects.

CHAPTER 2 Issues and Controversies Surrounding Growth Disorders

1. Human Growth Hormone Injections Benefit People with Growth Hormone Deficiencies 68
   Jane E. Brody
   Synthetic human growth hormone has recently garnered bad publicity because of its abuse by athletes, but it is of great benefit to children who suffer from a deficiency of natural growth hormone.

2. Human Growth Hormone Recipients May Be at Risk for Adrenal Crisis 74
   National Endocrine and Metabolic Diseases Information Service

People treated for human growth hormone deficiency and who also lack a certain pituitary hormone are at risk for developing an adrenal crisis that can cause death.

3. Early Puberty Is Linked to Environmental Toxins   80
Kim Ridley

The increase in precocious puberty—with some children showing signs of sexual development as early as the age of three—can be traced to endocrine-disrupting chemicals in pesticides, flame retardants, and plastic packaging.

4. Early Puberty Is Linked to Obesity   86
Joanna Dolgoff

There is no conclusive evidence proving that environmental chemicals contribute to early-onset puberty. Research does indicate that increasing rates of obesity play a major role in precocious puberty.

5. Little People Are Demeaned in Popular Culture   92
Lynn Harris

The dwarfism community in the United States is taking steps to counteract offensive portrayals of their members in the media and to promote positive language about people of short stature.

6. Acceptance of Dwarfism Is Preferable to Surgery   102
Dan Kennedy

It is important to view people with dwarfism as integral members of society instead of trying to "fix" people who are not broken.

7. Numerous Complications Are Associated with Limb-Lengthening Procedures — 107
   Little People of America Medical Advisory Board
   The possible complications of cosmetic limb-lengthening surgery include nerve injury, infection, fractures, unequal limb lengths, and osteoarthritis.

8. Genetic Research May Lead to the Prevention of Dwarfism — 112
   Phil Sneiderman
   An expert in biophysics is conducting research that could lay the groundwork for the future treatment or prevention of achondroplasia, the most common form of dwarfism.

CHAPTER 3 Living with Growth Disorders

1. A Mother with Marfan Syndrome Discusses Her Decision to Have Children — 119
   Lucy Hunter
   A mother describes her anguish upon discovering that she had passed along Marfan syndrome to her newborn son.

2. Little People Seek Tolerance — 125
   Janese Heavin
   Some people still find it acceptable to mock people with dwarfism, but there is nothing funny about the physical problems that often accompany this disorder.

3. Suffering Growth Hormone Deficiency as a Child — 128
   Anonymous
   A child relates how he was bullied for being short before his family learned about his growth hormone deficiency. Daily shots of growth hormone eventually enabled him to reach a normal height.

4. **The Impact of Turner Syndrome on a Young Woman**   **131**
   Collette

   The author describes the discrimination and prejudice she believes she has faced at school, at work, and on the street because of her Turner syndrome.

5. **A Pro Wrestler with a Growth Disorder Talks About the Price of Fame**   **135**
   Kent Babb

   At seven feet tall and 507 pounds, Paul Wight has had a lucrative and diverse career as a wrestler, actor, and businessman. But he lives with health problems that could shorten his life.

Glossary	**144**
Chronology	**147**
Organizations to Contact	**150**
For Further Reading	**155**
Index	**158**

FOREWORD

"Medicine, to produce health, has to examine disease."
—Plutarch

Independent research on a health issue is often the first step to complement discussions with a physician. But locating accurate, well-organized, understandable medical information can be a challenge. A simple Internet search on terms such as "cancer" or "diabetes," for example, returns an intimidating number of results. Sifting through the results can be daunting, particularly when some of the information is inconsistent or even contradictory. The Greenhaven Press series Perspectives on Diseases and Disorders offers a solution to the often overwhelming nature of researching diseases and disorders.

From the clinical to the personal, titles in the Perspectives on Diseases and Disorders series provide students and other researchers with authoritative, accessible information in unique anthologies that include basic information about the disease or disorder, controversial aspects of diagnosis and treatment, and first-person accounts of those impacted by the disease. The result is a well-rounded combination of primary and secondary sources that, together, provide the reader with a better understanding of the disease or disorder.

Each volume in Perspectives on Diseases and Disorders explores a particular disease or disorder in detail. Material for each volume is carefully selected from a wide range of sources, including encyclopedias, journals, newspapers, nonfiction books, speeches, government documents, pamphlets, organization newsletters, and position papers. Articles in the first chapter provide an authoritative, up-to-date overview that covers symptoms, causes and effects,

Foreword

treatments, cures, and medical advances. The second chapter presents a substantial number of opposing viewpoints on controversial treatments and other current debates relating to the volume topic. The third chapter offers a variety of personal perspectives on the disease or disorder. Patients, doctors, caregivers, and loved ones represent just some of the voices found in this narrative chapter.

Each Perspectives on Diseases and Disorders volume also includes:

- An **annotated table of contents** that provides a brief summary of each article in the volume.
- An **introduction** specific to the volume topic.
- Full-color **charts and graphs** to illustrate key points, concepts, and theories.
- Full-color **photos** that show aspects of the disease or disorder and enhance textual material.
- **"Fast Facts"** that highlight pertinent additional statistics and surprising points.
- A **glossary** providing users with definitions of important terms.
- A **chronology** of important dates relating to the disease or disorder.
- An annotated list of **organizations to contact** for students and other readers seeking additional information.
- A **bibliography** of additional books and periodicals for further research.
- A detailed **subject index** that allows readers to quickly find the information they need.

Whether a student researching a disorder, a patient recently diagnosed with a disease, or an individual who simply wants to learn more about a particular disease or disorder, a reader who turns to Perspectives on Diseases and Disorders will find a wealth of information in each volume that offers not only basic information, but also vigorous debate from multiple perspectives.

INTRODUCTION

The phrase *growth disorders* is used to describe a broad variety of conditions that manifest as abnormalities in growth and development. According to Mary Ruppe, author of *Diseases and Disorders*, malnutrition is the primary cause of one type of growth disorder—abnormally short stature—worldwide. The present volume, however, focuses on disorders that are intrinsic abnormalities rather than those resulting from food scarcity or chronic illnesses such as cystic fibrosis or sickle-cell anemia, which also affect growth. Most of the conditions classified here as disorders of growth are caused by chromosomal abnormalities, genetic mutations, endocrine system dysfunctions, or skeletal dysplasias (abnormal development). Gigantism, for example, which results from the body's secretion of too much growth hormone during childhood, is an endocrine system disorder. Turner syndrome, which causes short stature and incomplete puberty in girls, occurs when a female is born with a partial or completely missing X chromosome. Marfan syndrome, a condition that leads to an overproduction of connective tissue in various parts of the body, is an inherited genetic mutation. And dwarfism is an umbrella term for the more than two hundred conditions that manifest as skeletal dysplasias—an underdevelopment of bone in the limbs or in the trunk. What these intrinsically emerging growth disorders share in common is their relative rarity: They appear in fewer than one out of fifteen hundred live births.

Growth disorders were little understood until the twentieth century. Human growth hormone was first isolated from the pituitary gland in 1956, and it was not until 1984

Introduction

that scientists concluded that dwarfism is the result of a genetic mutation. Before the twentieth century, most people's exposure to those born with noticeable but rare growth disorders was through stories about—or exhibits of—human "oddities." "Freak shows," which were usually associated with traveling circuses and carnivals, were popular in Europe and the United States up through the middle of the twentieth century. Russian czar Peter the Great collected human biological rarities in the early 1700s, and Charles Stratton, the dwarf who became known as "Tom Thumb," was made famous by circus pioneer P.T. Barnum in 1843. As scientific advances began to reveal these sideshow anomalies as people with genetic mutations and diseases, "freaks" were perceived less as frightful monstrosities and more as individuals who deserved sympathy and respect. Laws were

Early growth disorder sufferers, such as Tom Thumb, were exhibited as human "oddities" in "freak shows" presented by traveling circuses and carnivals. (London Stereoscopic Company/Getty Images)

passed that restricted such entertainment, and the live traveling freak show fell into decline after 1940.

The appeal of the traveling freak show has perhaps found a popular new expression in modern documentaries and television reality shows such as *Little People, Big World*, which features a family headed by parents who both have dwarfism. The subjects of such series are typically shown in a sympathetic light, with storylines that highlight their challenges, their heroism, and their relationships with their families and friends. Thus, for the most part these shows are considered more respectable, even educational, in spite of their focus on human "oddities."

Another twenty-first-century development that could further alter popular perception of growth disorders is the 2011 discovery that some dwarfism-related genetic mutations may protect against serious illnesses that affect large numbers of people. For nearly twenty-five years, Ecuadoran endocrinologist Jaime Guevara-Aguirre has studied an extended family living in the Andes Mountains that carries a rare genetic abnormality known as Laron syndrome, a condition that prevents the body from using growth hormone. Laron syndrome is so rare that it is found in only about three hundred people worldwide. And out of the one hundred people in the remote Andean community who have it, Guevara-Aguirre and his colleagues discovered, none have developed diabetes, and only one has contracted a nonlethal cancer. These numbers are striking—in part because the high rate of obesity within this group would ordinarily lead to more cases of diabetes. Among the extended family members who do not exhibit Laron syndrome, 5 percent have been diagnosed with diabetes and 17 percent with cancer—rates similar to the overall Ecuadoran population, researchers note.

Nir Barzilai, director of the Institute for Aging Research at the Albert Einstein College of Medicine in New

York, asserts that the Ecuadoran study is an "important" finding that contributes to the study of the biology of aging and diseases related to aging. "In nature, dwarf models live longer," he says. "Ponies live longer than horses, small dogs live longer than large dogs. It's a very fascinating field in aging."[1]

American cell biologist Valter Longo, who teamed up with Guevara-Aguirre in the study of the Ecuadorans with Laron syndrome, has found evidence in tests on yeast, worms, and mice that limiting growth hormones could make these organisms live longer. In one study, the removal of a yeast gene that would be the equivalent of a human growth factor gene—in combination with a calorie-restricted "diet"—enabled the yeast to live ten times longer than normal. The implication is that reducing levels of growth hormones—genetically or through calorie restriction—increases longevity. In another experiment, the scientists exposed human cells in a petri dish to blood serum taken from people with Laron syndrome. They observed that the DNA in these cells was less likely to become damaged than was DNA in cells exposed to ordinary blood serum; moreover, when the DNA of the cells exposed to the Laron serum did become damaged, those cells were more likely to self-destruct than to reproduce. This, Longo states, appears to be a "double-protective" effect that might explain why people with Laron syndrome have a natural resistance to cancer.

While researchers remain unclear about why restricting growth hormones seems to prevent cell damage, Longo theorizes that it is because cells must expend energy in either growing and reproducing or in protecting themselves from injury, and, he explains, the cells of most people are stuck in "pro-growth" cycles.

Could growth hormone–blocking chemicals one day be used as a treatment for diabetes or as a cancer preventative? There is a possibility that a drug used to treat acromegaly (a form of gigantism) could prevent malignancies in people at high risk of cancer and in smokers, who tend to have high growth hormone levels. Animal trials have shown promise, but as this volume goes to press, clinical investigations in humans have yet to be conducted. Growth hormone–restricting treatments in people who have normal growth hormone levels can have serious side effects, so researchers remain cautious about pursuing such investigations.

The fact that Laron syndrome may one day provide a key to disease prevention and longevity suggests that there can be hidden gifts in what was once perceived as a freak-show "monstrosity." Genetic conditions that are typically defined as "disorders" might also be valued as anomalies harboring insights into the major health challenges of today. In the meantime, however, those who have growth disorders—and the people who care for them—still encounter great struggles in a world that often misunderstands or underestimates the day-to-day challenges of life as a person with dwarfism or Marfan syndrome or Turner syndrome. The publishers of *Perspectives on Diseases and Disorders: Growth Disorders* seek to enhance public awareness about these conditions by presenting descriptions of various growth disorders, approaches to treating and managing them, and personal viewpoints on their impact on those who live within these descriptions.

Notes
1. Lea Winerman, "Study: Dwarfism Gene May Offer Protection from Cancer, Diabetes," *PBS Newshour*, February 16, 2011. www.pbs.org.

CHAPTER 1
Understanding Growth Disorders

VIEWPOINT 1

Growth Disorders: An Overview

Neil Izenberg and Steven A. Dowshen

Growth disorders include conditions such as early or delayed puberty, skeletal dysplasia resulting in dwarfism, growth hormone deficiency, hypothyroidism, gigantism, and Cushing's syndrome, among others. Sometimes, a child's failure to grow normally is due to extrinsic factors such as exposure to nicotine or alcohol in the womb, poor nutrition, or chronic diseases like diabetes, cystic fibrosis, or sickle-cell anemia. But many conditions that are specifically identified as growth disorders are the result of heredity, genetic mutations, or abnormal production of hormones. For example, Turner syndrome, which leads to delayed puberty in girls, is caused by a chromosomal abnormality; Marfan syndrome, which leads to excessive growth and weakness of connective tissue, is an inherited condition.

Neil Izenberg, a pediatrician, is founder of the Nemours Center for Children's Health Media in Wilmington, Delaware. Steven A. Dowshen is a pediatric endocrinologist at the Alfred I. DuPont Hospital for Children in Wilmington, Delaware.

SOURCE: Neil Izenberg and Steven A. Dowshen, eds., "Growth Disorders," *Human Diseases and Conditions*, vol. 2, Charles Scribner's Sons, 2008. Copyright © 2008 Gale, a part of Cengage Learning, Inc. Reproduced by permission. www.cengage.com/permissions.

Photo on previous page. Dutchman Johann Albert Kramer, who was eight feet six inches tall, suffered from gigantism. The disorder results from the production of excessive amounts of growth hormone by the pituitary gland. (Science Source/Photo Researchers, Inc.)

Understanding Growth Disorders

When Jeremy turned eight, he looked like he was trapped inside the body of a four-year-old. "My friends teased me and called me 'Shorty,'" he said. "I felt terrible being so much shorter than my brother who was three years younger."

His parents took him to see a pediatric endocrinologist. The doctor took his medical history, blood tests, x-rays, and measurements. Jeremy's parents were told that his body was not making enough growth hormone. Daily shots of human growth hormone have helped Jeremy, and he is now taller than his brother.

What Is Normal Growth?

Everyone has a different size and shape, and there is a very wide range of what doctors consider "normal growth." In order to monitor growth, doctors use an established range of normal heights and weights for different age groups. From the time a child first goes to the doctor, measurements of height and weight are taken. The doctor uses a growth chart to compare a child's height and growth rate with those of others the same age. As a newborn, everyone starts out at about the same size. Yet, some end up short and some tall.

When developing a standard growth chart, researchers take a large number of children of different ages and make a graph of their heights and weights. The height at the 50th percentile means the height at which half of the children of that age are taller and half are shorter. The 25th percentile means that three quarters (75 percent) of the children are taller at that age, and one quarter (25 percent) are shorter. The 75th percentile means that three quarters of the children (75 percent) will be shorter and one quarter (25 percent) taller.

People vary greatly, and if children are between the 3rd and 97th percentile, and if they are growing at a normal rate, they usually are regarded as normal. If children are outside these ranges (over 97th percentile or under 3rd percentile), the doctor may look for some explanation. Most often, these children simply have inherited "short" or "tall" genes from their parents, and they will continue to grow at a normal pace.

Growth and Puberty

At the time of adolescence, a growth spurt normally occurs. Generally, growth spurts for girls start about two years earlier than growth spurts for boys. Rates of growth and change during puberty vary with the individual. Parents' growth and puberty patterns often are passed on through their genes to their children: If one or both parents had a late puberty, then their children are more likely to reach puberty later and to experience a later growth spurt. The medical term for this "late bloomer" pattern is constitutional growth delay.

The increase in growth rate that occurs during puberty is driven by the body's increase in production of sex hormones: estrogen from the ovaries in girls, and testosterone from the testicles in boys. These hormones cause the skeleton to grow and to mature more rapidly. Hormones produced by the adrenal glands at puberty contribute to the development of pubic hair (near the genitals) and underarm hair, but have little effect on bone growth. It follows, then, that disorders of pubertal development can affect a child's growth pattern and ultimate height. Pubertal disorders usually are grouped into two categories: precocious or premature puberty (which starts earlier than expected), and delayed or late puberty.

Precocious Puberty

In general, puberty is considered precocious (early) if changes in sexual development occur before age eight for girls and before age ten for boys. Most cases of precocious puberty result from the premature "switching on" of the puberty control center in the brain, located in the part of the brain called the hypothalamus. Hormones from the hypothalamus trigger the release of hormones from the pituitary gland (located at the base of the brain), which in turn stimulate the ovaries in girls and the testicles in boys to produce the higher levels of sex hormones needed to bring about the bodily changes of puberty.

Children with precocious puberty experience early growth spurts because of the abnormally early rise in sex hormone levels in their bodies. Although initially this causes these children to grow taller than others their age, their skeletons mature more rapidly, often causing them to stop growing at an early age. Therefore, if precocious puberty is left untreated, it may lead to a decrease in a child's ultimate height.

There are many possible causes for precocious puberty, including brain tumors and other disorders of the central nervous system; and tumors or other conditions that cause the gonads [sex glands] or adrenal glands to overproduce sex hormones. In girls, however, the majority of cases of precocious puberty are idiopathic, which means the precise cause is unknown.

Precocious puberty often can be treated effectively or controlled with medications that decrease the overproduction of sex hormones or that block their effects on the body. In many cases, this type of treatment can prevent or decrease the shortening of the child's ultimate height that would otherwise occur.

Delayed Puberty

Delayed puberty occurs when the hormonal changes of puberty occur later than normal, or not at all. Puberty is considered late if it has not begun by age 13 in girls or by age 15 in boys. Most children who experience delayed puberty are following the normal pattern called constitutional growth delay discussed previously.

Several medical conditions (such as disorders of the hypothalamus, pituitary, ovaries, and testicles) can result

Growth Disorders

in delayed puberty by interfering with the pubertal rise in sex hormones. Many chronic disorders of other body organs and systems (such as the intestines and lungs), as well as long-term treatments with certain medications (such as cortisone) also may cause delayed puberty.

As would be expected, children with delayed puberty do not experience growth spurts at the usual age, so they lag behind in height as their peers grow rapidly and mature sexually. When puberty finally occurs for these children, on its own or as a result of treatment, they "catch up": They may continue to grow into their late teens and may even exceed the final adult heights of some of their peers.

How Does Growth Take Place?

Growth occurs when bones of the arms, legs, and back increase in size. The long bones of the limbs have a growth plate at the end. The growth plate is made of cartilage, which is a tough, elastic tissue. Cartilage cells in the growth plate multiply and move down the bone to produce a matrix, or

This illustration shows bone growth as it progresses from the initial cartilage stage to become a fully-formed bone. The close-up shows osteoblasts, which are the cells responsible for bone growth.
(BSIP/Photo Researchers, Inc.)

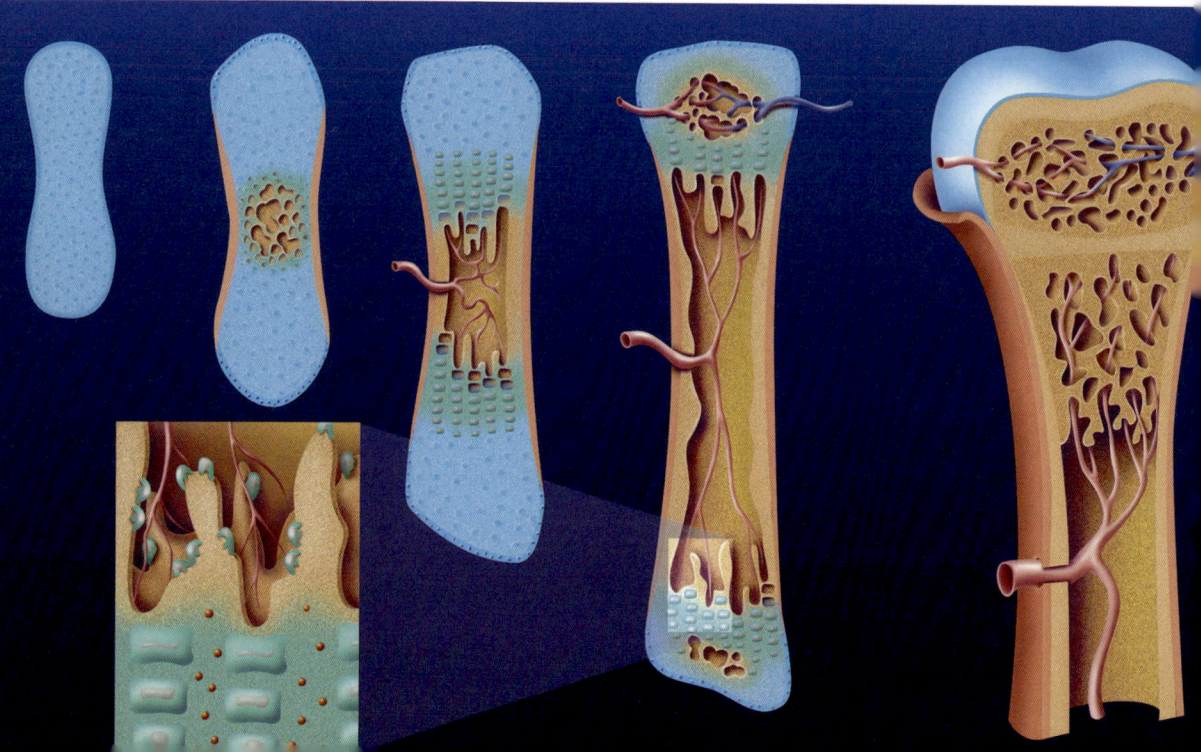

tissue from which new bone is formed. These cartilage cells then die, leaving spaces. Special cells called osteoblasts, meaning bone beginners, then produce bone (by laying down the minerals calcium and phosphorus) to fill the spaces and replace the matrix. Once all the cartilage in the growth plate has been turned to bone, growth stops. This usually occurs before ages 16 to 18. An x-ray of the hand or knee can show the doctor the bone age (maturity of the bone) and how much potential growth remains.

Why Do Some Children Not Grow Normally?

- *Nutrition.* Children with poor nutrition may have poor growth. A balanced diet and adequate protein are essential for normal growth. Some parts of the world have serious problems with malnutrition, and the growth of children may be affected in these areas.
- *Chronic diseases.* Chronic diseases that may impair growth include diabetes, congenital heart disorders, sickle cell disease, chronic kidney failure, cystic fibrosis, and rheumatoid arthritis.
- *Bone disorders.* One form of extreme short stature (height) is caused by abnormal formation and growth of cartilage and bone. Children with skeletal dysplasia or chondrodystrophies are short and have abnormal body proportions. Their intelligence levels usually are normal. Most of these conditions are inherited or occur due to genetic mutations (changes).
- *Intrauterine growth retardation (IUGR).* If growth in the uterus is interrupted while a fetus is forming or developing, the condition is called intrauterine (meaning within the uterus) growth retardation or IUGR. IUGR is not the same as when a baby is born prematurely. The small size of a premature infant usually is normal according to the gestational age (or the age from conception).

Failure to grow normally in the uterus may result from a problem with the placenta (the organ that supplies nutrients and oxygen to the baby). Growth of the fetus can be affected if the mother smokes cigarettes or drinks alcohol during the pregnancy. Infections, such as German measles, may cause the problem, and sometimes the cause cannot be determined.

- *Failure to thrive (FTT).* Failure to thrive (FTT), or inadequate weight gain anytime after birth, occurs frequently in infants. There are many possible causes, and the doctor must examine the child carefully. Often, the baby or child simply is not getting enough to eat. Sometimes there are other illnesses interfering with weight gain that must be treated.
- *Genetic conditions.* Several genetic conditions may involve problems with growth. One such condition is Turner syndrome. Girls with Turner syndrome have only one X chromosome or a second X chromosome that may be abnormal or incomplete. Affected girls are short and have underdeveloped ovaries.

Marfan syndrome is a hereditary condition affecting connective tissue and is associated with tall stature. People with Marfan syndrome have very long arms and legs, eye problems, and differences in facial features. Other physical problems, such as heart abnormalities, also may be present. It is commonly believed that Abraham Lincoln had Marfan syndrome.

Hormones and Growth Disorders

Growth is controlled by hormones (chemical messengers) from various glands. One of the most important, growth hormone, is secreted by the pituitary gland. The gland looks like a peanut sitting at the base of the brain. Other hormones also are essential for growth. The thyroid gland in the neck secretes thyroxine, a hormone required for normal bone growth. Sex hormones from the ovaries (estrogen) and

Stature for Age Percentile in Boys and Girls Ages 2 to 20 Years

Boys

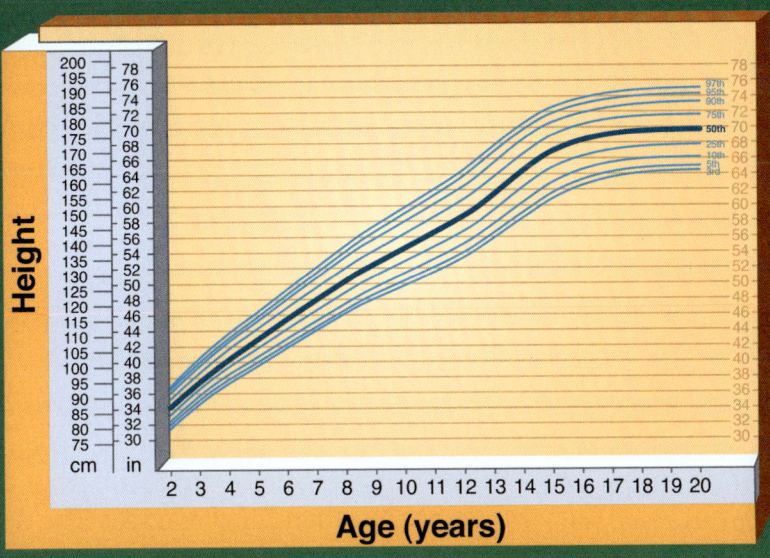

Girls

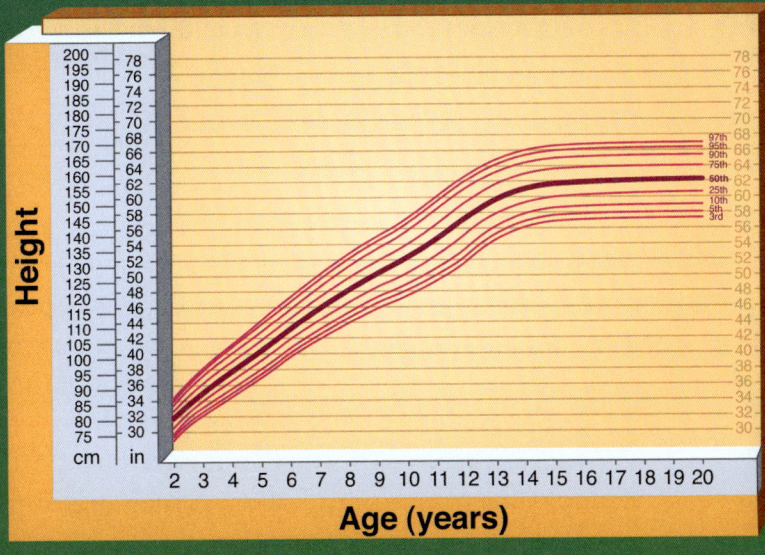

Developed by the National Center for Health Statistics in collaboration with the National Center for Chronic Disease Prevention and Health Promotion (2000).

Growth Disorders

testicles (testosterone) are essential for the growth spurt and other body changes that occur at puberty.

- *Pituitary hormones.* The pituitary gland is attached by a stalk to the hypothalamus, an area of the brain that controls the function of the pituitary. The anterior or front part of the pituitary gland secretes the following hormones that can affect growth:
  - Growth hormone to regulate bone growth
  - Thyroid-stimulating hormone to control the production and secretion of thyroid hormones
  - Gonad-stimulating hormones for development of the sex glands (gonads) and secretion of sex hormones
  - Adrenal-stimulating hormone to regulate the secretion of adrenal gland hormones.
- *Too little growth hormone (hypopituitarism).* Sometimes the pituitary gland does not make enough growth hormone. Usually, this will slow a child's growth rate to less than 2 inches a year. The deficiency may appear at any time during infancy or childhood. When doctors have ruled out other causes of growth failure, they may recommend special tests for growth hormone (GH) deficiency. Children with growth hormone deficiency are treated with daily injections of the hormone, often for a period of years. With early diagnosis and treatment, these children usually increase their rate of growth, and may catch up to achieve average or near-average height as adults.

In pituitary dwarfism, caused by low amounts of growth hormone, the person is short but has normal body proportions. This is different from other forms of dwarfism due to genetic skeletal dysplasias. In these cases, the person with dwarfism is short, and the growth of the arms, legs, torso, and head often is out of proportion. For example, the person's arms and legs may appear relatively smaller than the head or torso.

Understanding Growth Disorders

- *Too much growth hormone (hyperpituitarism).* Two conditions arise from excessive amounts of growth hormone in the body: acromegaly and gigantism. The cause usually is a benign pituitary tumor.

  Acromegaly, a condition caused by increased secretion of growth hormone after normal growth has been completed, occurs in adults. The condition is rare, occurring in 6 out of 100,000 people. Because the adult cannot grow taller, the excess growth hormone in acromegaly causes adult bones to thicken and other structures and organs to grow larger. Usually, it does not appear until middle age, when the person notes a tightening of a ring on the finger, or an increase in shoe size. Tests at that time may reveal a pituitary tumor.

  Gigantism occurs when excessive secretion of growth hormone occurs in children before normal growth has stopped. This results in the overgrowth of long bones. The vertical growth in height is accompanied by growth in muscle and organs. The result is a person who is very tall, with a large jaw, large face, large skull, and very large hands and feet. Many health problems may be associated with gigantism, including heart disease and vision problems. Delayed puberty also may occur in this condition. Surgery or radiation can correct the problem. Hormone replacement may be necessary if there is pituitary damage from this treatment.

> **FAST FACT**
>
> *Dysplasia* is a scientific term for abnormal growth or development. *Chondrodystrophy* refers to abnormal growth at the ends of the bones.

Thyroid and Adrenal Issues

- *Too little thyroid hormone (hypothyroidism).* The thyroid gland looks like a big butterfly at the base of the neck. One wing is on one side of the windpipe or trachea, and the other on the other side. The wings are joined by a thin strip of thyroid tissue. The thyroid gland makes the hormone thyroxine.

The thyroid is controlled by the pituitary gland, which makes thyroid-stimulating hormone. The hormone thyroxine controls the rate of chemical reactions (or metabolism) in the body. Too much thyroxine, or hyperthyroidism, speeds up metabolism.

Hypothyroidism is the opposite. Hypothyroidism is caused by the body's underproduction of thyroid hormone, and this affects many different body processes.

A child with thyroid hormone deficiency has slow growth and is physically and mentally sluggish. The lack of this hormone may be present at birth, if the thyroid gland did not develop properly in the fetus. Or the problem may develop during childhood or later in life as a result of certain diseases of the thyroid.

In most states, babies are tested for hypothyroidism at birth. Blood tests can detect the problem, and treatment usually is a daily pill that replaces the missing thyroid hormone. Early diagnosis and continuing treatment help these children grow and develop normally.

- *Too much cortisol (Cushing's syndrome).* The adrenal glands, which are located on top of the kidneys in the abdomen, secrete the hormone cortisol. If too much cortisol is made by the child's adrenals, or if large doses of the hormone are given to the child to treat certain diseases, Cushing's syndrome may develop. Children with this syndrome grow slowly, gain weight excessively, and may experience delayed puberty due to the effects of the abnormally large amounts of cortisol in the body.

A Complex Problem

There are many causes for growth problems. In order to detect these disorders early, it is important for doctors to track growth carefully in infants and children. Many of these conditions can be treated effectively, resulting in more normal adult heights for children with growth disorders.

VIEWPOINT 2

Achondroplasia: A Common Form of Dwarfism

Rebecca J. Frey

Achondroplasia, or short-limb dwarfism, is a genetic disorder affecting bone growth. As Rebecca J. Frey explains in the following selection, achondroplasia is caused by a gene that overproduces a protein that limits bone development. This results in skeletal abnormalities, including unusually short bones in the arms and legs. Other symptoms of achondroplasia include: abnormal skull structure, weak muscle tone, postural problems, bowed legs, breathing problems, and back pain. These symptoms can be managed through careful monitoring of the patient's growth, weight, and head size. On occasion, surgery may be needed to relieve pressure on the spinal cord, remove tonsils that block breathing, or correct bowed legs. Social support from groups such as Little People of America is strongly recommended for children with achondroplasia so that they can face the challenges of prejudice against people with dwarfism, the author asserts. Frey, a writer and contributor to medical reference texts, is the author of the *UXL Encyclopedia of Diseases and Disorders*.

SOURCE: Rebecca J. Frey, "Genetic Achondroplasia," *UXL Encyclopedia of Diseases and Disorders*, vol. 1, UXL, 2009. Copyright © 2009 Gale, a part of Cengage Learning, Inc. Reproduced by permission. www.cengage.com/permissions.

Growth Disorders

Achondroplasia, or short-limb dwarfism, is the most common form of abnormally short stature in adults. It is caused by a mutation in a single gene on chromosome 4 that regulates the conversion of cartilage to bone. This gene is the only gene that is known to be associated with achondroplasia.

Achondroplasia is basically a disorder of bone development. The skeleton of a human fetus is composed primarily of cartilage, a dense and somewhat elastic form of connective tissue that gradually turns to bone during normal development. In a person with achondroplasia, a gene that is involved in the process of bone formation produces too much of a protein that limits bone growth. As a result, the person with achondroplasia has unusually short bones in the arms and legs and other skeletal abnormalities. They also usually have difficulties with posture, joint disorders, and breathing problems in later life.

Demographics

Researchers estimate that achondroplasia occurs in one in every 15,000 to 40,000 live births. About 20 percent of cases are children who have one parent with achondroplasia; however, 75–80 percent of cases involve new mutations of the gene responsible for the disorder. These new mutations are more likely to occur in the sperm of fathers over 35; the mother's age does not matter, as far as is presently known. The disorder affects both sexes and all races equally.

The average adult height of people with achondroplasia is 4 feet 4 inches (1.3 meters) for men and 4 feet one-half inch (1.24 m) for women. The shortest living person with achondroplasia as of 2008 was Jyoti Amge, a teenager from Nagpur, India, who stands 23 inches (58 centimeters) tall and weighs 11 pounds (5 kilograms).

Causes and Symptoms

Achondroplasia is caused by a mutation in the FGFR3 gene on chromosome 4. A normal gene helps the body

Understanding Growth Disorders

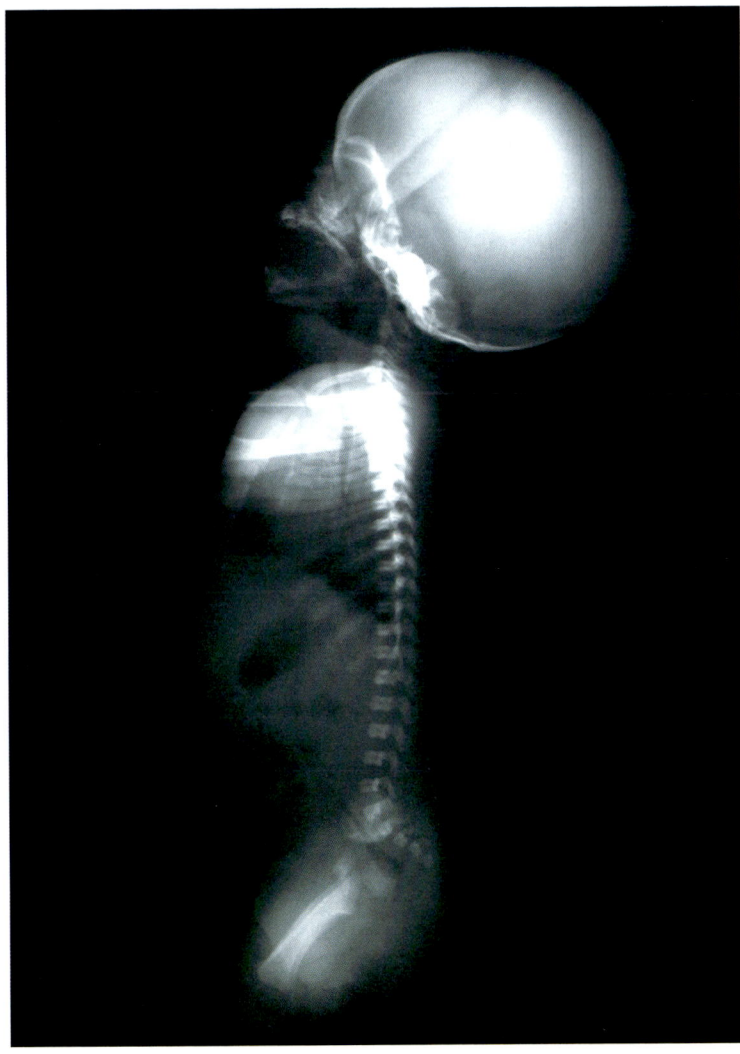

Achondroplasia is a genetic disorder that disturbs the normal growth of cartilage and is typically evident at birth. The condition is characterized by abnormal body proportions, and the limbs of affected individuals are very short in relation to the torso. (Scott Carmazine/Photo Researchers, Inc.)

convert cartilage to bone. The mutation in the gene related to achondroplasia results in severely shortened bones and weak muscle tone in the body.

The symptoms of achondroplasia are usually obvious by the first year of life. They include:
- Poor muscle tone.
- Slowness in learning to walk; a child with achondroplasia may not walk until some point between 24 and 35 months.

- Abnormal skull structure leading to frequent ear infections, apnea (temporary slowing or stopping of breathing), and overcrowding of the teeth.
- Distinctive facial features, particularly a prominent forehead and underdevelopment of the nose and midface.
- Greater than normal separation of the little finger from the ring finger, giving the hand a distinctive trident (three-pronged) shape.
- A tendency toward obesity.
- Postural problems, including a pronounced curvature of the spine in the lower back and bowed legs.
- Back and leg pain in adult life.

Babies with achondroplasia can be diagnosed before birth by ultrasound measurements of the growth of their long bones and head size. After birth, the diagnosis is usually based on x-ray studies of the child's bones and head size. The x-ray images usually reveal a small skull base, shortened growth plates in the long bones, square-shaped long bones, and normal-sized bones in the trunk area.

A genetic test can also be performed to confirm the diagnosis in children whose symptoms may be less clear....

Billy Barty

Billy Barty (1924–2000) was an Italian-American film actor who played in a number of movies from the 1930s through 2001. He also had roles in several television series, from *Alfred Hitchcock Presents* and *Peter Gunn* to *Little House on the Prairie* and *Frasier*. Born William John Bertanzetti in Millsboro, Pennsylvania, Barty became a noted spokesperson and activist tor persons with dwarfism.

In 1957 Barty gathered a group of others diagnosed with achondroplasia to meet with him in Reno, Nevada, to start an organization that would offer support and information to people with dwarfism and their families. Twenty-one people came to the meeting and formed Little

People of America (LPA), an organization that has over 6,000 members as of the early 2000s.

Barty was once asked in the 1970s why he worked so tirelessly to end stereotypes and ridicule of people with dwarfism. He said, "Most of us with dwarfism prefer to be described as 'Little People.' And please, put the emphasis on the word *People*. We did not spring from the pages of a story book or emerge from an enchanted forest. We are not magical beings and we are not monsters. We are parents and sons and daughters. We are doctors and lawyers and realtors and teachers. We dream, cry, laugh, shout, fall in love, and make mistakes. We are no different from you."

Treatment

The management of achondroplasia includes careful monitoring of the child's growth, head size, and weight pattern. There are special growth charts that doctors use to evaluate the rate of growth in children with achondroplasia. It is particularly important to prevent obesity if possible. In addition, children with achondroplasia need social support because of ongoing prejudice against people with dwarfism. Organizations such as Little People of America can offer helpful advice on the education and other future plans of children with achondroplasia.

Surgery may be performed if necessary to relieve pressure on the spinal cord or the brain. In some cases, there may be a buildup of fluid in the brain (hydrocephalus) that needs to be drained surgically. The child's tonsils and adenoids may be removed in order to lower the risk of apnea. The shape of bowed legs can be corrected surgically, but doctors disagree about the value of surgery intended to lengthen the legs.

Children with achondroplasia may need extra dental work because of the mismatch between the size of their

> **FAST FACT**
>
> One complication for dwarf infants is obstructive apnea—brief and repeated disruptions to breathing—which occurs when the airways are irregularly small.

teeth and the size of the jaw. In addition, they should be watched carefully for recurrent ear infections in order to minimize the risk of deafness and later learning difficulties.

There is disagreement among doctors as of the early 2000s regarding treatment with human growth hormone. It is considered an experimental treatment. Many doctors are concerned that using growth hormone in children with achondroplasia will lead to abnormal bone deposits and worsening of the spinal curvature.

Prognosis

The prognosis of a baby with achondroplasia depends on whether the defective gene is inherited from only one parent or from both. A child who inherits the gene from both parents will die before birth or shortly after birth from respiratory failure. About 3 percent of children with achondroplasia die suddenly and unexpectedly during the first year of life, usually from compression of the spinal cord.

A child who has one normal copy of the gene will usually have normal intelligence and abnormal life expectancy in spite of bone and joint problems.

The Future

There is no known way to prevent achondroplasia because the gene responsible for the condition can undergo mutation in families with no history of the disorder, and 75–80 percent of cases result from new mutations.

Although new mutations of the gene associated with achondroplasia cannot always be foreseen, people who have the condition should seek genetic counseling before marriage. If the partner does not have the mutation, there is a 50 percent chance with each pregnancy that the child will have achondroplasia. If both spouses have the mutation, they have a 25 percent chance of a normal child with each pregnancy, a 50 percent chance that the child will have achondroplasia, and a 25 percent chance that the child will die before or shortly after birth.

VIEWPOINT 3

Excessive Growth Hormone Leads to Gigantism and Acromegaly

National Endocrine and Metabolic Diseases Information Service

The following selection is provided by the National Endocrine and Metabolic Diseases Information Service, an educational arm of the National Institute of Diabetes and Digestive and Kidney Diseases, one of the National Institutes of Health. Acromegaly, the author explains, is a growth disorder caused by the body's overproduction of growth hormone (GH). In most cases, a benign pituitary gland tumor is the source of the GH overproduction, although GH-producing tumors may rarely occur in other parts of the body. In children, excessive GH results in gigantism, which leads to a sudden increase in growth rate and height. In adults, too much GH causes acromegaly, which can manifest as abnormal growth of the hands, feet, facial bones, and body organs. The first line of treatment for gigantism and acromegaly is usually surgical removal of the pituitary tumor, the authors note. Medication or radiation may be used instead of or in addition to surgery.

SOURCE: National Endocrine and Metabolic Diseases Information Services, "Acromegaly," May 2008, National Institutes of Health.

Growth Disorders

Acromegaly is a hormonal disorder that results from too much growth hormone (GH) in the body. The pituitary, a small gland in the brain, makes GH. In acromegaly, the pituitary produces excessive amounts of GH. Usually the excess GH comes from benign, or noncancerous, tumors on the pituitary. These benign tumors are called adenomas.

Acromegaly is most often diagnosed in middle-aged adults, although symptoms can appear at any age. If not treated, acromegaly can result in serious illness and premature death. Acromegaly is treatable in most patients, but because of its slow and often "sneaky" onset, it often is not diagnosed early or correctly. The most serious health consequences of acromegaly are type 2 diabetes, high blood pressure, increased risk of cardiovascular disease, and arthritis. Patients with acromegaly are also at increased risk for colon polyps, which may develop into colon cancer if not removed.

When GH-producing tumors occur in childhood, the disease that results is called gigantism rather than acromegaly. A child's height is determined by the length of the so-called long bones in the legs. In response to GH, these bones grow in length at the growth plates—areas near either end of the bone. Growth plates fuse after puberty, so the excessive GH production in adults does not result in increased height. However, prolonged exposure to excess GH before the growth plates fuse causes increased growth of the long bones and thus increased height. Pediatricians may become concerned about this possibility if a child's growth rate suddenly and markedly increases beyond what would be predicted by previous growth and how tall the child's parents are.

Symptoms of Acromegaly

The name acromegaly comes from the Greek words for "extremities" and "enlargement," reflecting one of its most common symptoms—the abnormal growth of the hands and feet. Swelling of the hands and feet is often an early feature, with patients noticing a change in ring or shoe size, particularly shoe width. Gradually, bone changes alter the patient's facial features: The brow and lower jaw protrude, the nasal bone enlarges, and the teeth space out.

Overgrowth of bone and cartilage often leads to arthritis. When tissue thickens, it may trap nerves, causing carpal tunnel syndrome, which results in numbness and weakness of the hands. Body organs, including the heart, may enlarge.

Other symptoms of acromegaly include
- joint aches
- thick, coarse, oily skin
- skin tags
- enlarged lips, nose, and tongue
- deepening of the voice due to enlarged sinuses and vocal cords
- sleep apnea—breaks in breathing during sleep due to obstruction of the airway
- excessive sweating and skin odor
- fatigue and weakness
- headaches
- impaired vision
- abnormalities of the menstrual cycle and sometimes breast discharge in women
- erectile dysfunction in men
- decreased libido

What Causes Acromegaly?

Acromegaly is caused by prolonged overproduction of GH by the pituitary gland. The pituitary produces several important hormones that control body functions such as growth and development, reproduction, and metabolism. But hormones never seem to act simply and directly. They usually "cascade" or flow in a series, affecting each other's production or release into the bloodstream.

Growth Disorders

GH is part of a cascade of hormones that, as the name implies, regulates the physical growth of the body. This cascade begins in a part of the brain called the hypothalamus. The hypothalamus makes hormones that regulate the pituitary. One of the hormones in the GH series, or "axis," is growth hormone–releasing hormone (GHRH), which stimulates the pituitary gland to produce GH.

Secretion of GH by the pituitary into the bloodstream stimulates the liver to produce another hormone called insulin-like growth factor I (IGF-I). IGF-I is what actually causes tissue growth in the body. High levels of IGF-I, in turn, signal the pituitary to reduce GH production.

The hypothalamus makes another hormone called somatostatin, which inhibits GH production and release. Normally, GHRH, somatostatin, GH, and IGF-I levels in the body are tightly regulated by each other and by sleep, exercise, stress, food intake, and blood sugar levels. If the pituitary continues to make GH independent of the normal regulatory mechanisms, the level of IGF-I continues to rise, leading to bone overgrowth and organ enlargement. High levels of IGF-I also cause changes in glucose (sugar) and lipid (fat) metabolism and can lead to diabetes, high blood pressure, and heart disease.

Pituitary Tumors

In more than 95 percent of people with acromegaly, a benign tumor of the pituitary gland, called an adenoma, produces excess GH. Pituitary tumors are labeled either micro- or macro-adenomas, depending on their size. Most GH-secreting tumors are macro-adenomas, meaning they are larger than 1 centimeter. Depending on their location, these larger tumors may compress surrounding brain structures. For example, a tumor growing upward may affect the optic chiasm—where the optic nerves cross—leading to visual problems and vision loss. If the tumor grows to the side, it may enter an area of the brain

Acromegaly Growth Hormone Levels

Normal

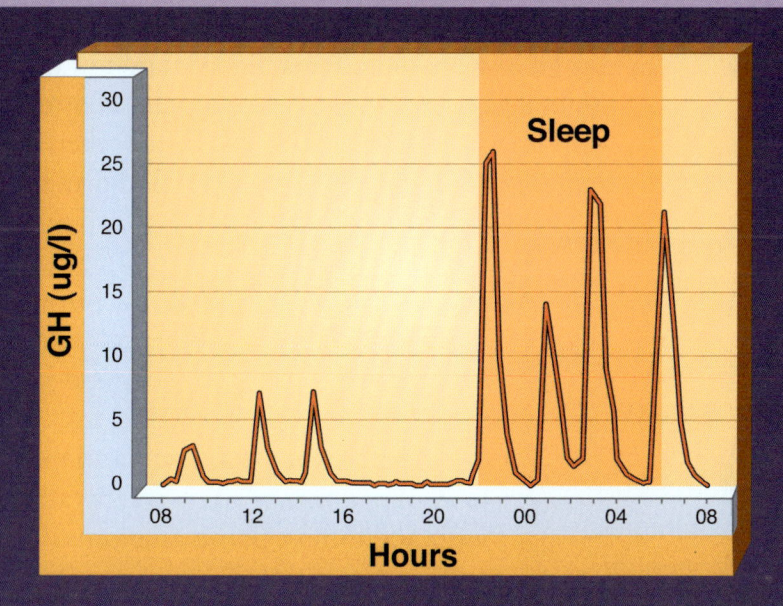

Acromegaly

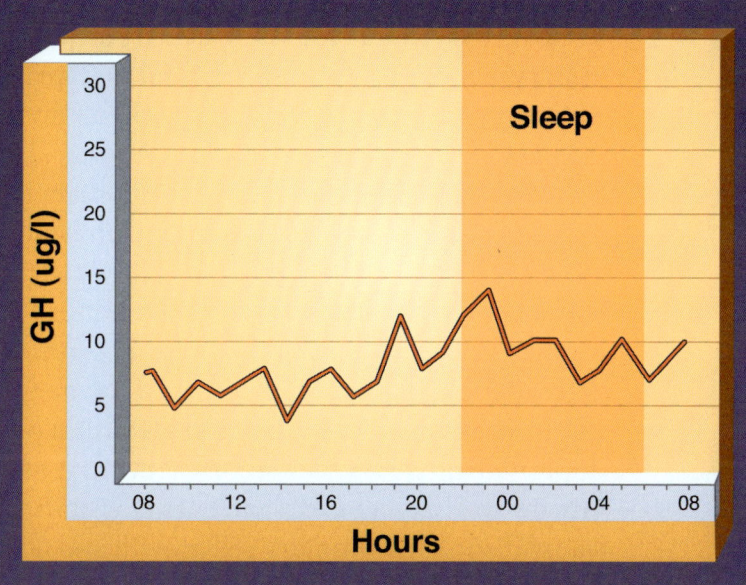

Taken from: Philip Chanson and Sylvie Salenave, "Acromegaly," *Orphanet Journal of Rare Diseases*, June 25, 2008.

Growth Disorders

called the cavernous sinus where there are many nerves, potentially damaging them.

Compression of the surrounding normal pituitary tissue can alter production of other hormones. These hormonal shifts can lead to changes in menstruation and breast discharge in women and erectile dysfunction in men. If the tumor affects the part of the pituitary that controls the thyroid —another hormone-producing gland—then thyroid hormones may decrease. Too little thyroid hormone can cause weight gain, fatigue, and hair and skin changes. If the tumor affects the part of the pituitary that controls the adrenal gland, the hormone cortisol may decrease. Too little cortisol can cause weight loss, dizziness, fatigue, low blood pressure, and nausea....

> **FAST FACT**
>
> A woman with acromegaly can produce breast milk even if she is not breast-feeding, according to the *Merck Manual of Medical Information*.

Rates of GH production and the aggressiveness of the tumor vary greatly among people with adenomas. Some adenomas grow slowly and symptoms of GH excess are often not noticed for many years. Other adenomas grow more rapidly and invade surrounding brain areas or the venous sinuses, which are located near the pituitary gland. Younger patients tend to have more aggressive tumors. Regardless of size, these tumors are always benign.

Most pituitary tumors develop spontaneously and are not genetically inherited. They are the result of a genetic alteration in a single pituitary cell, which leads to increased cell division and tumor formation. This genetic change, or mutation, is not present at birth, but happens later in life. The mutation occurs in a gene that regulates the transmission of chemical signals within pituitary cells. It permanently switches on the signal that tells the cell to divide and secrete GH. The events within the cell that cause disordered pituitary cell growth and GH oversecretion currently are the subject of intensive research.

Nonpituitary Tumors

Rarely, acromegaly is caused not by pituitary tumors but by tumors of the pancreas, lungs, and other parts of the brain. These tumors also lead to excess GH, either because they produce GH themselves or, more frequently, because they produce GHRH, the hormone that stimulates the pituitary to make GH. When these non-pituitary tumors are surgically removed, GH levels fall and the symptoms of acromegaly improve.

In patients with GHRH-producing, non-pituitary tumors, the pituitary still may be enlarged and may be mistaken for a tumor. Physicians should carefully analyze all "pituitary tumors" removed from patients with acromegaly so they do not overlook the rare possibility that a tumor elsewhere in the body is causing the disorder.

Diagnosing Acromegaly

Small pituitary adenomas are common, affecting about 17 percent of the population. However, research suggests most of these tumors do not cause symptoms and rarely produce excess GH. Scientists estimate that three to four out of every million people develop acromegaly each year and about 60 out of every million people suffer from the disease at any time. Because the clinical diagnosis of acromegaly is often missed, these numbers probably underestimate the frequency of the disease.

Blood tests. If acromegaly is suspected, a doctor must measure the GH level in a person's blood to determine if it is elevated. However, a single measurement of an elevated blood GH level is not enough to diagnose acromegaly: Because GH is secreted by the pituitary in impulses, or spurts, its concentration in the blood can vary widely from minute to minute. At a given moment, a person with acromegaly may have a normal GH level, whereas a GH level in a healthy person may even be five times higher.

Growth Disorders

More accurate information is obtained when GH is measured under conditions that normally suppress GH secretion. Health care professionals often use the oral glucose tolerance test to diagnose acromegaly because drinking 75 to 100 grams of glucose solution lowers blood GH levels to less than 1 nanogram per milliliter (ng/ml) in healthy people. In people with GH overproduction, this suppression does not occur. The oral glucose tolerance test is a highly reliable method for confirming a diagnosis of acromegaly....

Imaging. After acromegaly has been diagnosed by measuring GH or IGF-I levels, a magnetic resonance imaging (MRI) scan of the pituitary is used to locate and detect the size of the tumor causing GH overproduction. MRI is the most sensitive imaging technique, but computerized tomography (CT) scans can be used if the patient should not have MRI. For example, people who have pacemakers or other types of implants containing metal should not have an MRI scan because MRI machines contain powerful magnets.

If a head scan fails to detect a pituitary tumor, the physician should look for non-pituitary "ectopic" tumors in the chest, abdomen, or pelvis as the cause of excess GH. The presence of such tumors usually can be diagnosed by measuring GHRH in the blood and by a CT scan of possible tumor sites.

Rarely, a pituitary tumor secreting GH may be too tiny to detect even with a sensitive MRI scan.

Treatment for Acromegaly

Currently, treatment options include surgical removal of the tumor, medical therapy, and radiation therapy of the pituitary.

Goals of treatment are to
- reduce excess hormone production to normal levels
- relieve the pressure that the growing pituitary tumor

Understanding Growth Disorders

may be exerting on the surrounding brain areas
- preserve normal pituitary function or treat hormone deficiencies
- improve the symptoms of acromegaly

Surgery. Surgery is the first option recommended for most people with acromegaly, as it is often a rapid and effective treatment. The surgeon reaches the pituitary via an incision through the nose or inside the upper lip and, with special tools, removes the tumor tissue in a procedure called transsphenoidal surgery. This procedure promptly relieves the pressure on the surrounding brain regions and leads to a rapid lowering of GH levels. If the surgery is successful, facial appearance and soft tissue swelling improve within a few days.

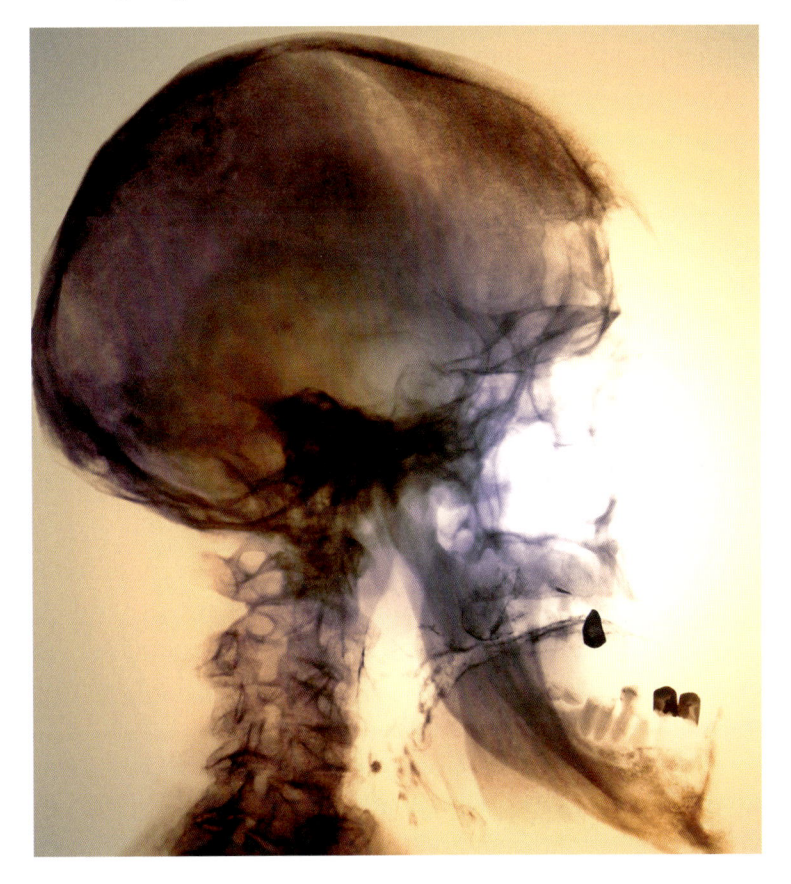

A colored X-ray of a skull shows acromegaly. This growth disorder results from the chronic production of excessive growth hormone, which causes uncontrolled enlargement of the hands, feet, and jaw, as well as a lengthening of facial features. (Zephyr/Photo Researchers, Inc.)

PERSPECTIVES ON DISEASES AND DISORDERS

Surgery is most successful in patients with blood GH levels below 45 ng/ml before the operation and with pituitary tumors no larger than 10 millimeters (mm) in diameter. Success depends in large part on the skill and experience of the surgeon, as well as the location of the tumor. Even with the most experienced neurosurgeon, the chance of a cure is small if the tumor has extended into critical brain structures or into the cavernous sinus where surgery could be risky.

The success rate also depends on what level of GH is defined as a cure. The best measure of surgical success is normalization of GH and IGF-I levels. The overall rate of remission—control of the disease—after surgery ranges from 55 to 80 percent....

Even when surgery is successful and hormone levels return to normal, people with acromegaly must be carefully monitored for years for possible recurrence of the disease. More commonly, hormone levels improve, but do not return to normal. Additional treatment, usually medications, may be required.

Medical therapy. Medical therapy is most often used if surgery does not result in a cure and sometimes to shrink large tumors before surgery. Three medication groups are used to treat acromegaly.

Somatostatin analogs (SSAs) are the first medication group used to treat acromegaly. They shut off GH production and are effective in lowering GH and IGF-I levels in 50 to 70 percent of patients. SSAs also reduce tumor size in around 0 to 50 percent of patients but only to a modest degree. Several studies have shown that SSAs are safe and effective for long-term treatment and in treating patients with acromegaly caused by nonpituitary tumors. Long-acting SSAs are given by intramuscular injection once a month....

The second medication group is the GH receptor antagonists (GHRAs), which interfere with the action of GH. They normalize IGF-I levels in more than 90 percent of patients. They do not, however, lower GH levels. Given once a day through injection, GHRAs are usually well-tolerated by patients. The long-term effects of these drugs on tumor growth are still under study. Side effects can include headaches, fatigue, and abnormal liver function.

Dopamine agonists make up the third medication group. These drugs are not as effective as the other medications at lowering GH or IGF-I levels, and they normalize IGF-I levels in only a minority of patients. Dopamine agonists are sometimes effective in patients who have mild degrees of excess GH and have both acromegaly and hyperprolactinemia—too much of the hormone prolactin. Dopamine agonists can be used in combination with SSAs. Side effects can include nausea, headache, and lightheadedness.

Radiation Therapy

Radiation therapy is usually reserved for people who have some tumor remaining after surgery and do not respond to medications. Because radiation leads to a slow lowering of GH and IGF-I levels, these patients often also receive medication to lower hormone levels. The full effect of this therapy may not occur for many years.

The two types of radiation delivery are conventional and stereotactic. Conventional radiation delivery targets the tumor with external beams but can damage surrounding tissue. The treatment delivers small doses of radiation multiple times over 4 to 6 weeks, giving normal tissue time to heal between treatments.

Stereotactic delivery allows precise targeting of a high-dose beam of radiation at the tumor from varying angles. The patient must wear a rigid head frame to keep the head still. The types of stereotactic radiation delivery currently available are proton beam, linear accelerator (LINAC), and gamma knife. With stereotactic delivery, the tumor must be at least 5 mm from the optic chiasm to prevent radiation damage. This treatment can sometimes be done in a single session, reducing the risk of damage to surrounding tissue.

All forms of radiation therapy cause a gradual decline in production of other pituitary hormones over time, resulting in the need for hormone replacement in most patients. Radiation also can impair a patient's fertility. Vision loss and brain injury are rare complications. Rarely, secondary tumors can develop many years later in areas that were in the path of the radiation beam.

Which Treatment Is Most Effective?

No single treatment is effective for all patients. Treatment should be individualized, and often combined, depending on patient characteristics such as age and tumor size.

If the tumor has not yet invaded surrounding nonpituitary tissues, removal of the pituitary adenoma by an experienced neurosurgeon is usually the first choice. Even if a cure is not possible, surgery may be performed if the patient has symptoms of neurological problems such as loss of peripheral vision or cranial nerve problems. After surgery, hormone levels are measured to determine whether a cure has been achieved. This determination can take up to 8 weeks because IGF-I lasts a long time in the body's circulation. If cured, a patient must be monitored for a long time for increasing GH levels.

If surgery does not normalize hormone levels or a relapse occurs, an endocrinologist should recommend additional drug therapy. With each medication, long-term therapy is necessary because their withdrawal can lead to rising GH levels and tumor re-expansion.

Radiation therapy is generally reserved for patients whose tumors are not completely removed by surgery, who are not good candidates for surgery because of other health problems, or who do not respond adequately to surgery and medication.

VIEWPOINT 4

Diagnosing and Treating Marfan Syndrome

March of Dimes Foundation

Marfan syndrome is an inheritable growth disorder that causes connective tissue abnormalities, the March of Dimes Foundation explains in the following article. A mutation in the gene that produces the protein fillibrin results in an overgrowth and weakness of connective tissue, which can adversely affect crucial areas of the body. Individuals with this disorder are often tall and have unusually long faces, arms, legs, fingers, and toes. Some serious health challenges can result from Marfan syndrome, including heart problems, skeletal abnormalities, breathing difficulties, and visual troubles. In spite of these challenges, the life expectancy for people with Marfan syndrome has greatly improved due to earlier diagnosis and advances in treatment. Medications and corrective surgery offer effective treatments for heart, lung, and eye problems in Marfan patients.

Founded in 1938, the March of Dimes Foundation is a nonprofit organization dedicated to reducing and treating birth defects.

SOURCE: March of Dimes, "Marfan Syndrome," marchofdimes.com, January 2009. Copyright © 2009 by March of Dimes. Reprinted by permission.

Growth Disorders

Marfan syndrome is a genetic disorder that affects connective tissue. Connective tissue holds other tissues together. Because connective tissue is found throughout the body, Marfan syndrome can affect many body systems, including the heart, blood vessels, bones, eyes, lungs and skin. It does not affect intelligence. Signs and symptoms of Marfan syndrome can be mild or severe. They may be present at birth or become apparent in childhood or in adult life.

Marfan syndrome affects more than 200,000 Americans (about 1 in 5,000 to 1 in 10,000). The disorder affects males and females of all races and ethnic groups. The condition is named for Dr. Antoine Marfan who, in 1896, described a 5-year-old girl with unusually long, slender fingers and limbs and other skeletal abnormalities.

Effects of Marfan Syndrome

Many affected individuals are tall, slender and loose-jointed. Arms, legs, fingers and toes often are unusually long. Some people with Marfan syndrome have low foot

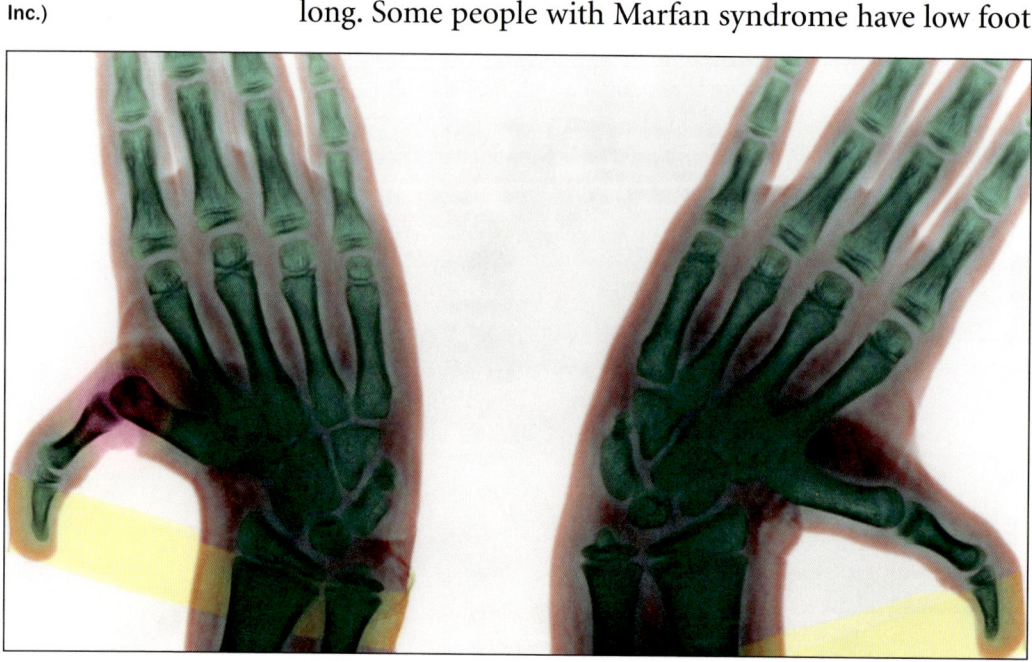

A colored X-ray displays the hands of a patient with Marfan syndrome, a rare genetic disorder affecting connective tissue. Those afflicted become very tall and thin in stature and may have very long fingers. (CNRI/Photo Researchers, Inc.)

46   PERSPECTIVES ON DISEASES AND DISORDERS

arches (flat feet), and others have high arches. Individuals with Marfan syndrome usually have long, narrow faces, and their teeth are generally crowded.

Individuals with Marfan syndrome can have one or more of the problems described below. The severity of the effects of Marfan syndrome varies greatly, even within the same family.

- *Heart and blood vessel problems:* The most serious problem associated with Marfan syndrome is weakness of the wall of the aorta. The aorta is the body's largest artery, which carries oxygen-rich blood from the left side of the heart to the rest of the body.

In Marfan syndrome, the wall of the aorta gradually weakens and stretches (aortic dilation). Eventually, this can cause a tear (dissection) in the lining of the aorta. Blood can leak out through the tear into the aortic wall, sometimes causing a rupture that allows blood to leak into the chest or abdomen. If not detected and treated, these complications can cause sudden death.

- *Abnormal heart valves:* Heart valves are tiny flaps or gates that keep the blood flowing in one direction through the heart. With Marfan syndrome, the heart's mitral valve tends to be large and floppy (mitral valve prolapse). An abnormal mitral valve can allow blood to briefly flow backwards during a heartbeat. Sometimes this creates an abnormal sound (heart murmur) that a health care provider may hear through a stethoscope. Mitral valve prolapse can sometimes be associated with irregular or rapid heartbeat and shortness of breath.
- *Skeletal abnormalities:* Many affected individuals have a lateral (sideways) curve of the spine called scoliosis. Sometimes there is a sharp, forward curvature called kyphosis. Many individuals have a breastbone that protrudes outward (called pectus carinatum) or sinks inward (called pectus excavatum). These chest

Growth Disorders

abnormalities can sometimes affect heart or lung function.

Sometimes the connective tissue that surrounds the spinal cord loosens and stretches out. This condition is called dural ectasia and can cause pain in the lower back or legs and numbness or weakness in the legs.

- *Lung problems:* Persons with Marfan syndrome sometimes develop breathing problems, such as shortness of breath. Breathing problems may result from skeletal abnormalities that do not allow the chest to fully expand or from sudden collapse of the lungs (called spontaneous pneumothorax).

Adults with Marfan syndrome are at increased risk for early emphysema, a breathing disorder usually associated with smoking, even if they don't smoke. Individuals with Marfan syndrome also may have short pauses in breathing during sleep, called sleep apnea.

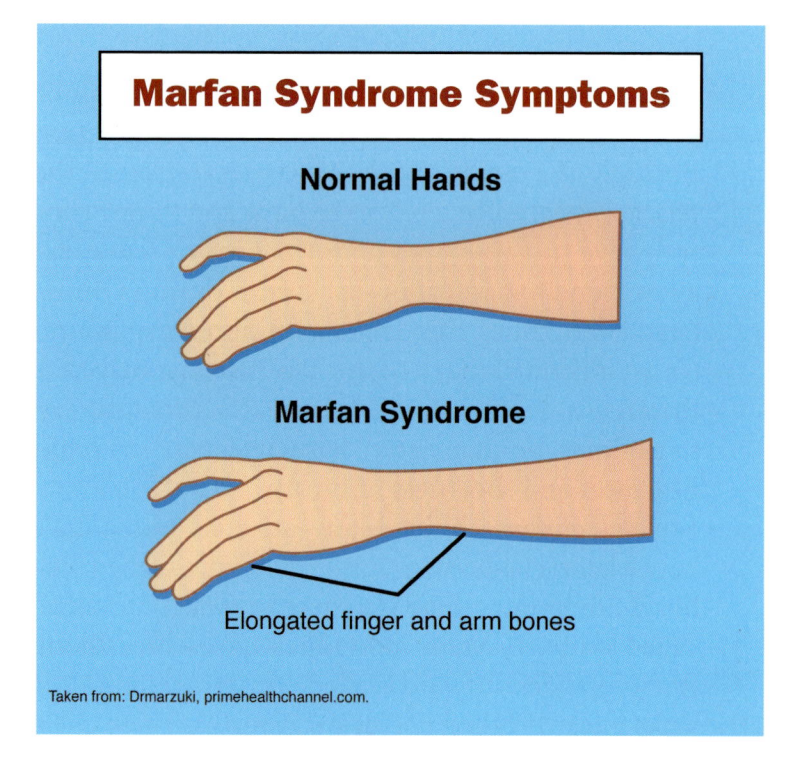

Marfan Syndrome Symptoms

Normal Hands

Marfan Syndrome

Elongated finger and arm bones

Taken from: Drmarzuki, primehealthchannel.com.

- *Eye problems:* The lens of one or both eyes is off-center in more than 60 percent of persons with Marfan syndrome. This is called ectopia lentis. Most affected individuals are nearsighted and have astigmatism (the eyes cannot focus clearly).

Individuals with Marfan syndrome are at increased risk for detachment of the retina (tears in the light-sensing lining at the back of the eye), cataracts (clouding of the lens of the eye) and glaucoma (increased pressure in the eye). Individuals with Marfan syndrome often develop cataracts and glaucoma at an earlier age than individuals in the general population. Retinal detachment and glaucoma can lead to vision loss.

How Marfan Syndrome Is Diagnosed

An evaluation for Marfan syndrome generally includes:
- A complete physical examination.
- An eye examination by an ophthalmologist (eye doctor). The ophthalmologist uses eye drops to fully dilate the pupils of the eyes and examines them with a slit-lamp (a microscope with a light attached) to look for lens dislocation.
- Heart tests, including an electrocardiogram (EKG) and an echocardiogram. An EKG measures electrical activity in the heart. An echocardiogram is a noninvasive ultrasound that lets doctors look for involvement of the heart and blood vessels. Imaging tests, such as a computed tomography (CT scan) or magnetic resonance imaging (MRI), may be used to check the condition of the aorta.
- A family history to determine if there are other family members known or suspected to have Marfan syndrome and/or who died early due to an unexplained heart disorder or an aneurysm. An aneurysm is a bulging of a blood vessel, such as the aorta, that sometimes can cause the vessel to rupture.

- Genetic testing of a blood sample to help confirm the diagnosis.
- An MRI of the lower spine to look for dural ectasia.

Treatment for Marfan Patients

Advances in treatment have greatly improved the outlook for children and adults with Marfan syndrome. Today, the life expectancy of individuals with the disorder who receive proper treatment is about 70 years.

Most of the problems associated with Marfan syndrome can be managed effectively, as long as they are diagnosed early. The disorder usually is treated by a team of experienced physicians and health care professionals, overseen by a single doctor who knows all of its aspects.

The team of physicians should include a cardiologist (heart doctor). Affected individuals need to have a series of echocardiograms (called serial echocardiograms) to measure the dimensions of the aorta and check the condition of the heart valves. These and other tests help the doctors determine whether or not treatment is needed and when intervention should take place.

Addressing Heart Problems

To help prevent or reduce heart problems, doctors often recommend treatment with high blood pressure medications called beta blockers. These medications reduce the strength and frequency of heartbeats, reducing stress on the wall of the aorta. Studies suggest that beta blockers may slow down the rate of dilation of the aorta and help prevent it from tearing. Individuals who cannot tolerate beta blockers are sometimes treated with other high blood pressure medications, such as calcium channel blockers or angiotensin-converting enzyme inhibitors.

New studies suggest that high blood pressure medications called angiotensin-receptor blockers may help prevent or even reverse aortic dilation. Larger studies are under way to test the effectiveness of these drugs.

In spite of the use of medication, the aorta sometimes continues to dilate. Doctors recommend surgery to repair the aorta before there is a danger of it tearing or dissecting. Doctors evaluate a number of factors when considering surgery and planning its timing. These factors include the size of the aorta and the rate at which it is dilating, family history of aortic dilation/dissection, and whether the aortic valve is leaking.

Surgical Options

There are a few surgical options for repairing the aorta. In one operation, the surgeon replaces a section of the aorta with a synthetic tube (called a composite graft) and sometimes repairs or replaces the aortic valve. More recently, some individuals with Marfan syndrome have had a valve-sparing procedure in which the aortic valve is retained and a portion of the aorta closest to the heart is replaced.

Individuals with Marfan syndrome should have aortic surgery performed at a hospital where the surgeons are experienced with Marfan syndrome. Affected individuals should discuss the pros and cons of various surgical options with their surgeon.

Early preventive surgery for aortic dilation is safer than waiting until emergency surgery is needed. A 1999 study showed that with preventive surgery, the death rate was 1.5 percent vs. 12 percent for patients who had emergency surgery.

When necessary, other faulty heart valves can be surgically repaired or replaced. After any valve replacement surgery, the individual must take anti-clotting medication for life, because blood tends to clot when it comes in contact with artificial valves.

Individuals with Marfan syndrome who have had surgery to replace a heart valve or have certain heart abnormalities are prone to heart wall or heart valve infections. They must be treated with oral antibiotics to prevent infection

Growth Disorders

before dental procedures (including cleaning, filling and extractions) that may release bacteria into the bloodstream. All individuals with Marfan syndrome should check with their cardiologist to see if they need antibiotics before dental procedures.

Sometimes individuals with Marfan syndrome who have had repair of the upper portion of the aorta have enlargement of other parts of their aortas. These individuals need to be followed with serial echocardiograms and a CT scan or MRI of the chest, abdomen and pelvis at least yearly. In some cases, surgical repair may be needed.

Other Marfan-Related Issues

How are skeletal problems treated? Children and adolescents with Marfan syndrome are monitored yearly for signs of scoliosis. Many develop mild scoliosis, which may not require treatment.

In more severe or progressive cases, scoliosis can cause back pain and shortness of breath. In these cases, a brace or surgery is recommended. Bracing can sometimes halt the progression of scoliosis, although sometimes surgery is needed to correct the deformity.

Chest wall (pectus) abnormalities also can interfere with breathing. Corrective surgery can be performed to alleviate these symptoms.

How are eye problems treated? Children and adults with Marfan syndrome should have a yearly eye examination by an ophthalmologist. Most eye problems, such as nearsightedness, can be corrected with glasses or contact lenses. Early treatment for cataracts and glaucoma usually can prevent or lessen vision problems. Detached retinas can be treated with lasers.

Can individuals with Marfan syndrome exercise? Most individuals can benefit from mild forms of exercise. However, strenuous exercise can place stress on the aorta. Therefore, children and adults with Marfan syndrome should avoid strenuous exercise, including competitive, collision and contact sports. Heavy lifting also should be avoided. With their doctor's guidance, many can participate in less vigorous activities, such as walking, slow jogging, playing golf, leisurely bicycle riding, swimming and slow-paced tennis.

What Causes Marfan Syndrome?

Marfan syndrome is caused by mutations (changes) in one member of a pair of genes called the fibrillin genes. These genes are located on chromosome 15, one of the 23 pairs of human chromosomes.

Normally, the fibrillin gene enables the body to produce fibrillin, a protein that is a crucial component of connective tissue. Fibrillin normally is an abundant component of the connective tissue found in the aorta, in the ligaments that hold the eye's lenses in place, in bones and in the lungs.

Mutations in the fibrillin gene lead to the formation of insufficient or faulty fibrillin, which probably weakens connective tissue. Fibrillin also helps regulate the levels of a growth factor (called transforming growth factor-beta) that plays a role in tissue growth and repair. Recent studies suggest that excessive amounts of this growth factor are released in individuals with Marfan syndrome, contributing to the signs and symptoms of the disorder.

An Inheritable Disorder

The mutated fibrillin gene usually is inherited from one parent who has Marfan syndrome. The mutation is a dominant genetic trait. This means that each child of a parent with Marfan syndrome has a 50 percent chance of inheriting the mutation and a 50 percent chance of not inheriting it. Only those children who inherit the mutation develop the signs and symptoms of Marfan syndrome.

About 25 percent of cases of Marfan syndrome are sporadic. This means that they are caused by a new mutation

Growth Disorders

that occurred by chance in one of the fibrillin genes in a sperm or egg cell of an unaffected parent. Parents who themselves do not have Marfan syndrome and do not have a family history of Marfan syndrome, but who have an affected child, should meet with a genetic counselor to discuss their risks in another pregnancy.

As with other inherited disorders, Marfan syndrome cannot be caught from another person. Although it may be diagnosed at any age, the signs and symptoms of Marfan syndrome do not occur unless the person has the mutation.

Pregnancy and Marfan Syndrome

There are several important issues for women with Marfan syndrome who are considering pregnancy. There is a 50 percent chance of having a child with Marfan syndrome with each pregnancy. In addition, the stress of pregnancy may cause rapid enlargement of the aorta, especially if the aorta is significantly enlarged before pregnancy. The risk of the aorta tearing is low, but not zero, in women with Marfan syndrome who have a normal aortic size. The risk increases during pregnancy as the aorta enlarges.

Women with Marfan syndrome should consult their health care providers and their cardiologist before pregnancy to discuss whether pregnancy is safe for them. The cardiologist generally recommends an echocardiogram to determine the dimensions of the aorta.

During pregnancy, an affected woman should receive prenatal care from a high-risk obstetrician who has experience with Marfan syndrome. She should also see her cardiologist regularly. She needs to have an echocardiogram in the first, second and third trimesters to monitor the size of her aorta. If the aorta measures less than 4 cm, there is a low risk of tears during pregnancy.

> **FAST FACT**
>
> Famous historical figures who likely had Marfan syndrome include Pharaoh Akhenhaten; Mary, Queen of Scots; Charles de Gaulle; and Abraham Lincoln.

Women who are taking a beta-blocker generally can safely continue taking the medication throughout pregnancy. Those who have had a valve replaced usually are on an oral blood thinner called coumadin (warfarin). Because this drug increases the risk of birth defects, pregnant women are switched to another blood thinner called heparin, which is given by injection (usually two or three times a day), during pregnancy.

Women with Marfan syndrome do not appear to have an increased risk of miscarriage. Most women with Marfan syndrome can have a vaginal delivery. The doctor will take appropriate measures to lessen the stress of labor and birth. However, if the woman has significant aortic dilation, a cesarean birth may be recommended.

A woman with Marfan syndrome should have a follow-up echocardiogram at 1 to 2 months after delivery to check the size of her aorta.

Prevention

At present, there is no way to prevent Marfan syndrome. Early diagnosis can help prevent serious complications. Genetic counseling enables informed decisions about childbearing and provides up-to-date information about the genetic basis of Marfan syndrome and genetic testing for this condition.

VIEWPOINT 5

Turner Syndrome: A Chromosomal Deficit Exclusive to Girls

Turner Syndrome Society of the United States

Named for the endocrinologist Henry Turner, who published a famous description of the disorder in the 1930s, Turner syndrome (TS) is a condition in which a female child is born with one X chromosome (rather than two) or is missing part of one X chromosome. This syndrome leads to short stature and to infertility due to early ovarian failure. Treatment with hormone replacement therapy enables girls with TS to have a pubertal growth spurt and develop a mature female body. Some of the effects of TS vary from individual to individual, with 30 percent of patients experiencing heart, thyroid, and kidney abnormalities. TS patients may also experience nonverbal learning disabilities, scoliosis, and hearing loss. This selection was prepared by the Turner Syndrome Society of the United States, a nonprofit organization that provides health-related resources to TS patients, families, and physicians.

SOURCE: Turner Syndrome Society of the United States, "What Is Turner Syndrome?," http://www.turnersyndrome.org. Copyright © Turner Syndrome Society of the United States. All rights reserved. Reproduced by permission.

Understanding Growth Disorders

Turner syndrome (TS) is a chromosomal condition that describes girls and women with common features that are caused by complete or partial absence of the second sex chromosome. The syndrome is named after Dr. Henry Turner, who was among the first to describe its features in the 1930's. TS occurs in approximately 1 of every 2,000 female births and in as many as 10% of all miscarriages.

Diagnosis is made through a test called a karyotype, which is usually performed on cells in the amniotic fluid before birth and on cells in the blood after birth. A trained specialist counts the chromosomes in the white blood cells and looks for abnormalities.

Primary Characteristics of Turner Syndrome

Short Stature. The most common feature of Turner syndrome is short stature. The average height of an adult TS woman who has not received human growth hormone treatment is 4'8". Individuals tend to be a little shorter at birth, averaging 18.5" compared to an average of 20" for all girls. Growth failure continues after birth, and most girls with TS fall below the normal female growth curve for height during early childhood. TS girls who are not treated with hormone replacement usually do not have a pubertal growth spurt; many will continue to grow at a slow rate until they are in their twenties. Many girls who undergo growth hormone treatment have been able to achieve adult height within the lower range of normal.

Premature Ovarian Failure. Most (90%) TS individuals will experience early ovarian failure. In the general population, the ovaries produce eggs and hormones necessary for

> **FAST FACT**
>
> Girls and women with Turner syndrome have a higher risk of developing celiac disease, an immune-system reactivity to gluten, the protein in wheat and other grains.

Average Height: Turner vs. Non-Turner

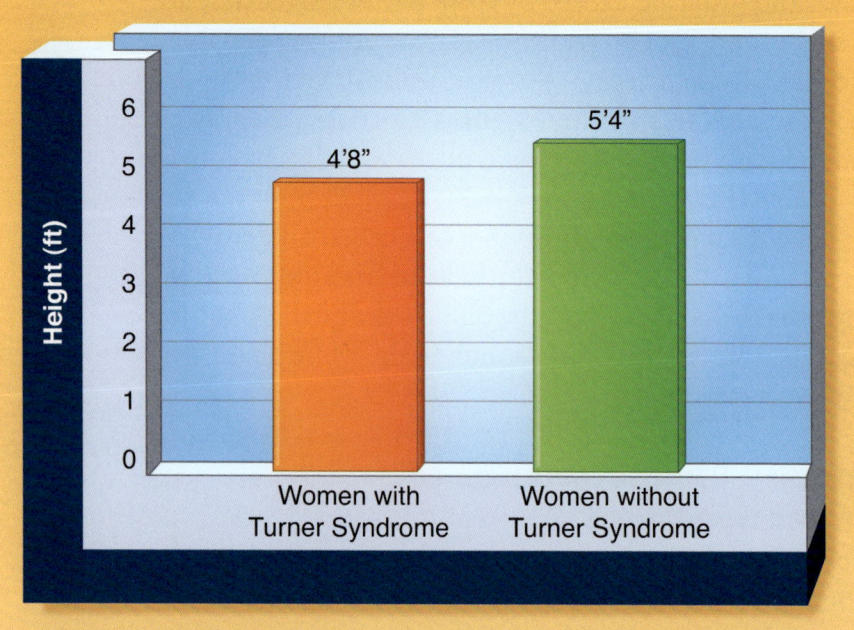

	Women with Turner Syndrome	Women without Turner Syndrome
Height	4'8"	5'4"

Taken from: National Center for Health Statistics and suite101.com.

the development of secondary sexual characteristics. Estrogen replacement therapy is necessary for breast development, feminine body contours, menstruation and proper bone development. About a third of TS individuals will show some signs of breast development without estrogen treatment; however, many will not complete puberty, and those that do often have premature ovarian failure. Therefore, the majority of individuals will require estrogen from puberty until the normal age of menopause. Fertility without assisted reproduction therapy is rare.

Cognitive Processes

TS individuals are on average of normal overall intelligence with the same variance as the general population. They do, however, often have difficulty with spatial-temporal processing (imagining objects in relation to each other), nonverbal memory and attention. This may cause problems with math, sense of direction, manual dexterity and social skills. New and better ways to compensate for these problems, which currently fall under the general category of nonverbal learning disabilities, are being researched.

Physical Features

Many characteristic features are associated with Turner syndrome. Their presence and severity vary greatly from individual to individual.

- Narrow, high-arched palate (roof of the mouth)
- Retrognathia (receding lower jaw)
- Low-set ears
- Low hairline (the hair on the neck is closer to the shoulders)
- Webbed neck (excess or stretched skin)
- Slight droop to eyes
- Strabismus (lazy eye)
- Broad chest
- Cubitus valgus (arms that turn out slightly at the elbows)
- Scoliosis (curvature of the spine)
- Flat feet
- Small, narrow fingernails and toenails that turn up (usually if lymphedema was present at birth)
- Short fourth metacarpals (the ends of these bones form the knuckles)
- Edema (swelling) of hands and feet, especially at birth

Associated Risks

Several medical problems occur more frequently in individuals with Turner syndrome than in the general population. It is important that TS individuals are screened regularly to see if any of these problems exist. Most of

Growth Disorders

A light micrograph of the karyotype of chromosomes from a patient with Turner syndrome. In healthy women there would be two X chromosomes instead of one, seen at lower right. (SPL/Photo Researchers, Inc.)

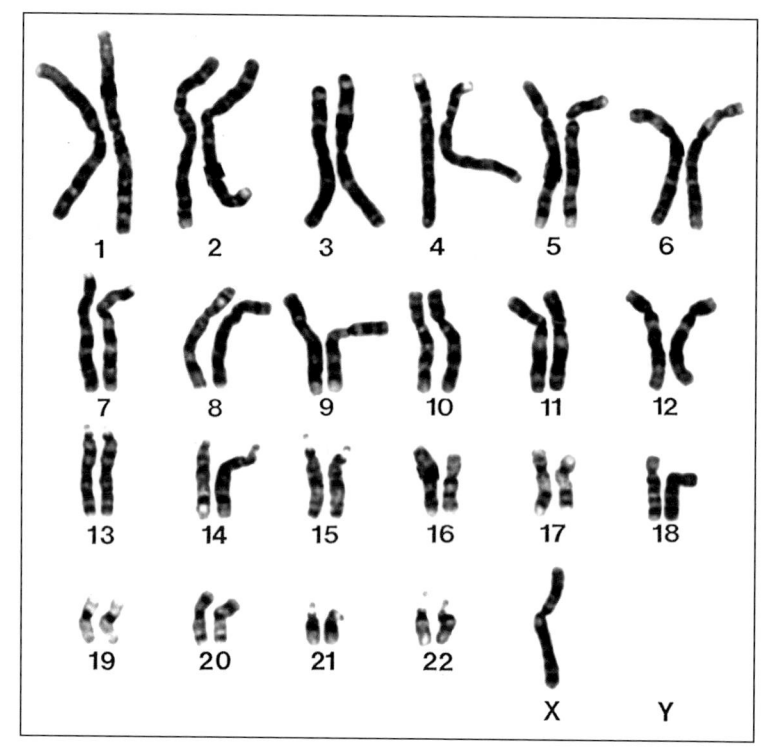

these conditions can be managed successfully with good medical care.

Heart. Some form of cardiac abnormality occurs in approximately one-third of TS patients. Problems are primarily left-sided and may include:

- Coarctation (narrowing) of the aorta and bicuspid aortic valve (a valve with two leaflets instead of the usual three).
- TS individuals are also at higher risk for hypertension, or high blood pressure.
- TS patients should receive an echocardiogram or MRI [magnetic resonance imaging] to evaluate the heart at the time of diagnosis regardless of age and have their hearts re-evaluated periodically for aortic root enlargement.
- All individuals with TS should be aware of the symptoms of dissection of the aorta, an uncommon but

life-threatening complication. These include sudden, severe, sharp, stabbing, tearing, or ripping chest pain, intense anxiety, rapid pulse, profuse sweating, nausea and vomiting, dizziness, fainting or shortness of breath.

Kidney. Thirty percent of TS individuals will have kidney abnormalities. Many of the abnormalities do not cause any medical problems; however, some may result in urinary tract infections and an increased risk of hypertension. It is recommended that TS individuals receive a renal [kidney] ultrasound examination at the time of diagnosis.

Thyroid. Hypothyroidism (low level of thyroid hormone) caused by autoimmune thyroiditis (inflammation of thyroid gland) occurs frequently in individuals with TS. It can be diagnosed with a blood test and is easily treated with thyroid hormone.

Ears. Otitis media (ear infection) is extremely common in TS girls, particularly in infancy and early childhood. Aggressive treatment of infections is appropriate. The majority (50–90%) of TS women will also develop early sensorineural (nerve) hearing loss and may require hearing aids earlier than the general population.

VIEWPOINT 6

The Use and Abuse of Growth Hormone

The Hormone Foundation

Produced by the pituitary gland, human growth hormone controls the body's metabolism, increases height and muscle mass, and decreases body fat. An injectable synthetic form of growth hormone (GH) is used to treat conditions such as GH deficiency, short stature, and muscle wasting caused by HIV infection. Some people use growth hormone illegally to improve athletic performance or to lose body fat, but GH abuse may lead to serious and potentially dangerous side effects, including muscle and joint pain, hepatitis, and heart disease. GH is safe and effective only when prescribed by a physician for specific disorders, the author maintains. This selection is provided by the Hormone Foundation, the public education affiliate of the Endocrine Society, which helps to raise public awareness about hormone-related conditions.

SOURCE: Linn Goldberg, Alan D. Rogol, and Peter, H. Sonksen, "Growth Hormone: Use and Abuse," Hormone Foundation, June 2009. Copyright © 2009 by Hormone Foundation. All rights reserved. Reproduced by permission.

Understanding Growth Disorders

Human growth hormone (GH) is a substance that regulates your body's growth and metabolism. GH is made by the pituitary gland, located at the base of the brain. GH helps children grow taller (also called linear growth), increases muscle mass, and decreases body fat. In both children and adults, GH helps control the body's metabolism—the process by which cells change food into energy and make other substances needed by the body.

If children or adults have too much or too little GH, they may have health problems. Growth hormone deficiency (too little GH) and some other health problems can

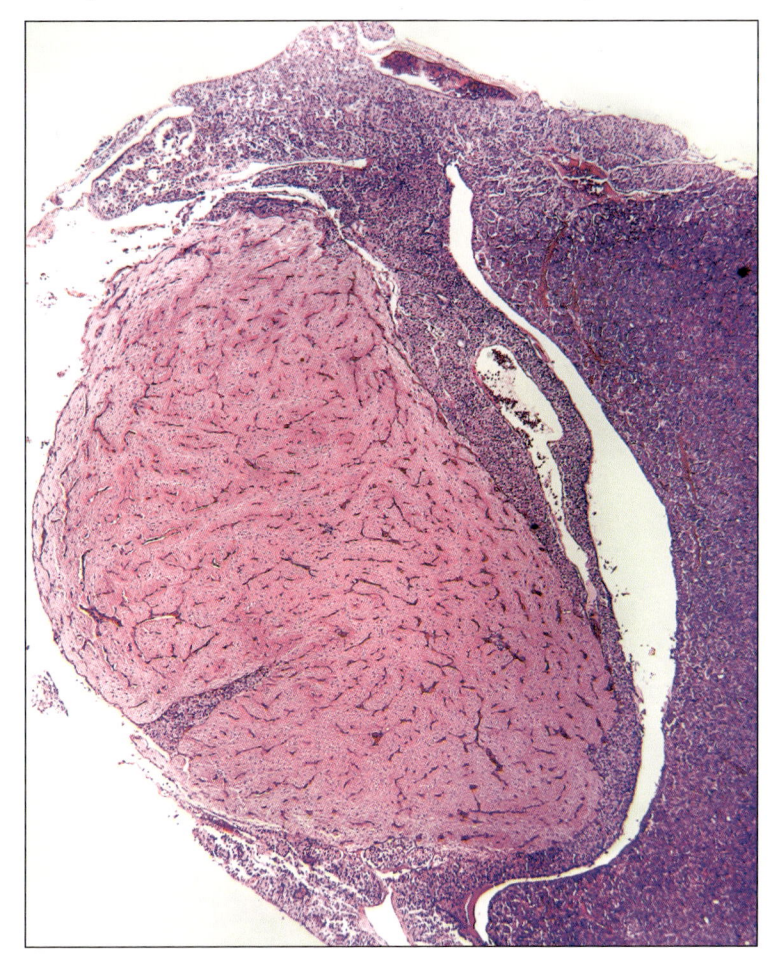

A light micrograph shows the three tissue types that make up the pituitary gland. Human growth hormone, produced by the gland, controls the body's metabolism and can increase height and muscle mass and decrease body fat. **(Garry DeLong/Photo Researchers, Inc.)**

Growth Disorders

be treated with synthetic (manufactured) GH. Sometimes GH is used illegally for non-medical purposes.

Growth Hormone Therapy

The United States (US) Food and Drug Administration (FDA) has approved GH treatment for specific conditions. GH is only available by prescription and is injected.

In children, GH is used to treat
- growth hormone deficiency
- conditions that cause *short stature* (being shorter than children of the same age), such as chronic kidney disease, Turner syndrome, and Prader-Willi syndrome

"3:45 pm: Ignoring its squeals of protest, I have injected the lab rat with the growth hormone drug."

Cartoon by Richard Jolley. Cartoonstock.com.

In adults, GH is used to treat
- growth hormone deficiency
- muscle wasting (loss of muscle tissue) from HIV
- short bowel syndrome

In addition to these uses, doctors outside of the US sometimes prescribe GH for other conditions. (When doctors prescribe medicines for conditions other than the ones officially approved, the process is called "off-label" use.)

Growth Hormone Use by Healthy Adults

Studies of healthy adults taking GH have produced conflicting results. Some short-term studies showed that older adults increased their endurance and strength, with increased muscle and decreased fat mass. But other studies did not show similar benefits. More studies are needed to fully understand the benefits and risks of GH use in healthy adults.

Aside from its use in research studies, prescribing or using GH off-label is illegal in the US. Adults can achieve improved health, body composition, strength, and endurance by following a healthy diet and getting regular exercise.

How Is Growth Hormone Abused?

People sometimes take GH illegally to stop or reverse the effects of aging or to improve athletic performance. Some athletes believe taking GH alone will not achieve the desired results, so they take it along with anabolic (tissue-building) steroids in an effort to build muscle, increase strength, and decrease body fat. Some athletes also use insulin to increase the muscular effects of GH, which is a dangerous practice because it lowers blood sugar.

People can experience harmful side effects when they abuse GH. Side effects of short-term use include joint and muscle pain, fluid build-up, and swelling in the joints. If GH

> **FAST FACT**
>
> The US Department of Health and Human Services stopped distributing human growth hormone in 1985 after learning that three people being treated with it died of a brain disorder akin to "mad cow" disease.

is injected with shared needles, people may be exposed to HIV, AIDS, or hepatitis. Taking high doses of GH over a long period of time may contribute to heart disease. GH sold illegally may contain unknown and potentially harmful ingredients. For example, if people take GH derived from human tissue, they risk developing a fatal brain condition called Creutzfeldt-Jakob disease, a condition similar to mad cow disease.

Some companies sell human GH pills or GH releasers, claiming that the pills are "anti-aging" substances. But these substances have not been proven to increase the body's production of GH or to fight aging, increase muscle, or provide other benefits. GH has no effect if it's taken as a pill because it is inactivated during digestion.

Key Things to Remember
- Synthetic GH is safe and effective when used for certain conditions approved by the FDA.
  - GH must be prescribed by a physician.
  - Abuse of GH can have serious side effects.
  - Healthy adults can improve their health and fitness with diet and exercise.
  - If you're worried about GH deficiency in yourself or a family member, talk with a doctor.

CHAPTER 2

Issues and Controversies Surrounding Growth Disorders

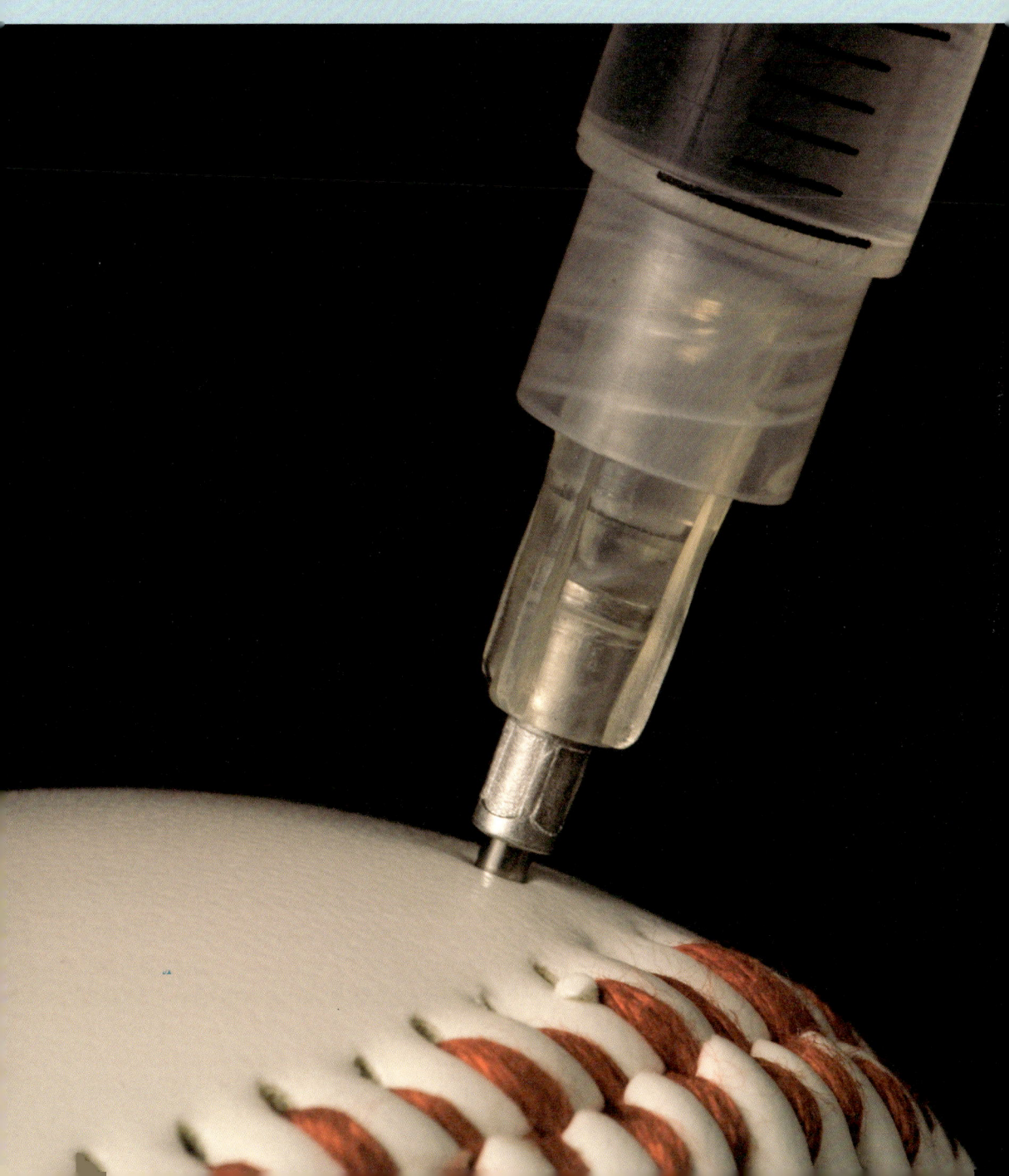

VIEWPOINT 1

Human Growth Hormone Injections Benefit People with Growth Hormone Deficiency

Jane E. Brody

Daily injections of synthetic growth hormone (GH) are of great benefit to children who have a deficiency of natural growth hormone, writes Jane E. Brody in the following article. People with GH deficiencies often have fragile bones, low muscle mass, and excessive abdominal fat. Several years of childhood and adolescent GH therapy increases muscle mass and bone density as well as height in such people. Many experts suggest continuing GH therapy even after adult height has been reached to help prevent obesity and to ensure that bone density remains within the normal range, the author notes. GH therapy may also be of benefit to children who have other disorders that adversely affect body composition, such as cystic fibrosis, Prader-Willi syndrome, and juvenile arthritis.

Photo on previous page. The injection of human growth hormone has recently received adverse publicity because of its illegal use by athletes attemptinig to improve their performance. However, it is of great benefit to children who suffer from growth hormone deficiency. (© Jason Satterwhite/ Alamy)

SOURCE: Jane E. Brody, "A Plus Side for Human Growth Hormone," *New York Times*, May 4, 2010. Copyright © 2010 by New York Times. All rights reserved. Reproduced by permission.

Human growth hormone has acquired a bad reputation, thanks to athletes who have abused it in their quest for stardom. But for tens of thousands of children whose growth and development are stymied by a deficiency of growth hormone, daily injections of this biologically synthesized growth stimulant can put them on track toward normality.

I'm not talking about children with normal hormone levels whose genetic heritage will keep them well below the average height for American men and women (respectively, 5 feet 9 inches and just under 5 feet 4), although they, too, can sometimes benefit from an artificial boost from the hormone.

According to Dr. Judith L. Ross, a pediatric endocrinologist at Jefferson University Hospitals in Philadelphia, even hormonally normal children genetically destined to be short can gain one and a half to perhaps four inches in final height, depending on when treatment is begun. Thus, a boy who would otherwise top out at 5 feet 3 could conceivably reach 5 feet 7 through hormone therapy begun at an early age, well before puberty.

But the claims for human growth hormone have been considerably overstated, perhaps because it is such a profitable product, costing tens of thousands of dollars a year—only sometimes covered by insurance. "Many kids who are not actually growth-hormone-deficient will not respond to the treatment, so it is a very expensive crapshoot," Dr. Philippa Gordon, a pediatrician in Brooklyn, told me in an e-mail message. "What is the psychological fallout when the parents have spent $30,000 a year and the child fails to grow? Also, the long-term side effects are not known."

Who Can Benefit?

Although treatment of hormonally normal children is still highly controversial, therapy is clearly indicated for those with a diagnosed deficiency in growth hormone, which

Growth Disorders

> ### What Endocrinologists Do
>
> Endocrinologists are trained to diagnose and treat hormone imbalances and problems by helping to restore the normal balance of hormones in your system. They take care of many conditions including:
>
> - diabetes
> - thyroid diseases
> - metabolic disorders
> - over- or underproduction of hormones
> - menopause
> - osteoporosis
> - hypertension
> - cholesterol (lipid) disorders
> - infertility
> - lack of growth (short stature)
> - cancers of the endocrine glands
>
> Source: The Hormone Foundation, 2011.

has health benefits beyond height stimulation, according to a report by Dr. Ross and colleagues in the April [2010] issue of the journal *Pediatrics*.

At age 14, Cutler Dozier of Minneapolis was 4 feet 10 inches and weighed 76 pounds, smaller than the average 12-year-old and showing no signs of puberty. His mother, Phyllis Dozier, said she had long thought his size was because of his extremely premature birth. Then, she said in an interview, she learned that "while most preemies eventually catch up, Cutler was falling further and further behind."

"He was growing only one-quarter to one-half inch a year," she added, "whereas most children grow about two inches a year."

Although Cutler's pediatrician was surprisingly unconcerned, Mrs. Dozier wisely insisted on a referral to a pediatric endocrinologist, who found that Cutler had a serious growth hormone deficiency. He strongly recommended treatment (80 percent of the cost was covered by insurance, leaving the family with a $535 monthly co-payment) and in just one year of daily hormone injections, Cutler grew four and a half inches. His mother said, "At 15, although he was still small for his age, he was finally on the chart for a 15-year-old."

She added: "Not only did he get taller, his appetite really picked up and his hands grew bigger. He reached 5 feet 4 inches at age 16 but had not yet completed puberty, so the endocrinologist recommended he continue treatment. We left the decision up to Cutler, who decided to continue injecting the hormone for four more years."

Now 22 and fully grown, Cutler weighs 140 pounds and stands a confident 5 feet 9 inches.

Improving Body Composition and Proportions

Dr. Ross says that other children who can benefit from growth hormone therapy are those who were born small for their gestational age and who fail to catch up by age 2 or so; girls born with a chromosomal abnormality called Turner syndrome; and children with genetic disorders called SHOX deficiency and Noonan syndrome.

The *Pediatrics* authors wrote that "short children who were born small for gestational age have relatively large hands and feet and relatively broad shoulders and pelvis." But six years of hormone therapy can help to normalize their body proportions.

Other conditions still under study for possible benefits from growth hormone therapy include Prader-Willi syndrome, which can result in extreme obesity; cystic fibrosis; and juvenile arthritis that is treated

> **FAST FACT**
> Somatropin is a biosynthetic human growth hormone that is injected under the fat of a patient's skin to treat growth hormone deficiency.

Growth Disorders

with steroids. In each of these disorders, the researchers reported, growth hormone therapy may improve body composition.

Children who are deficient in growth hormone tend to accumulate body fat, especially around the abdomen, and develop more fragile bones and abnormally low muscle mass. Treating them with the hormone reverses these effects, and results in increased bone density and improved muscle mass in the arms, legs and trunk.

Continued Therapy Throughout Adolescence

Still, the levels can remain below normal even after six years of treatment. Two studies have shown that further improvement in body composition can result if growth hormone therapy is continued for several years after a child reaches adult height.

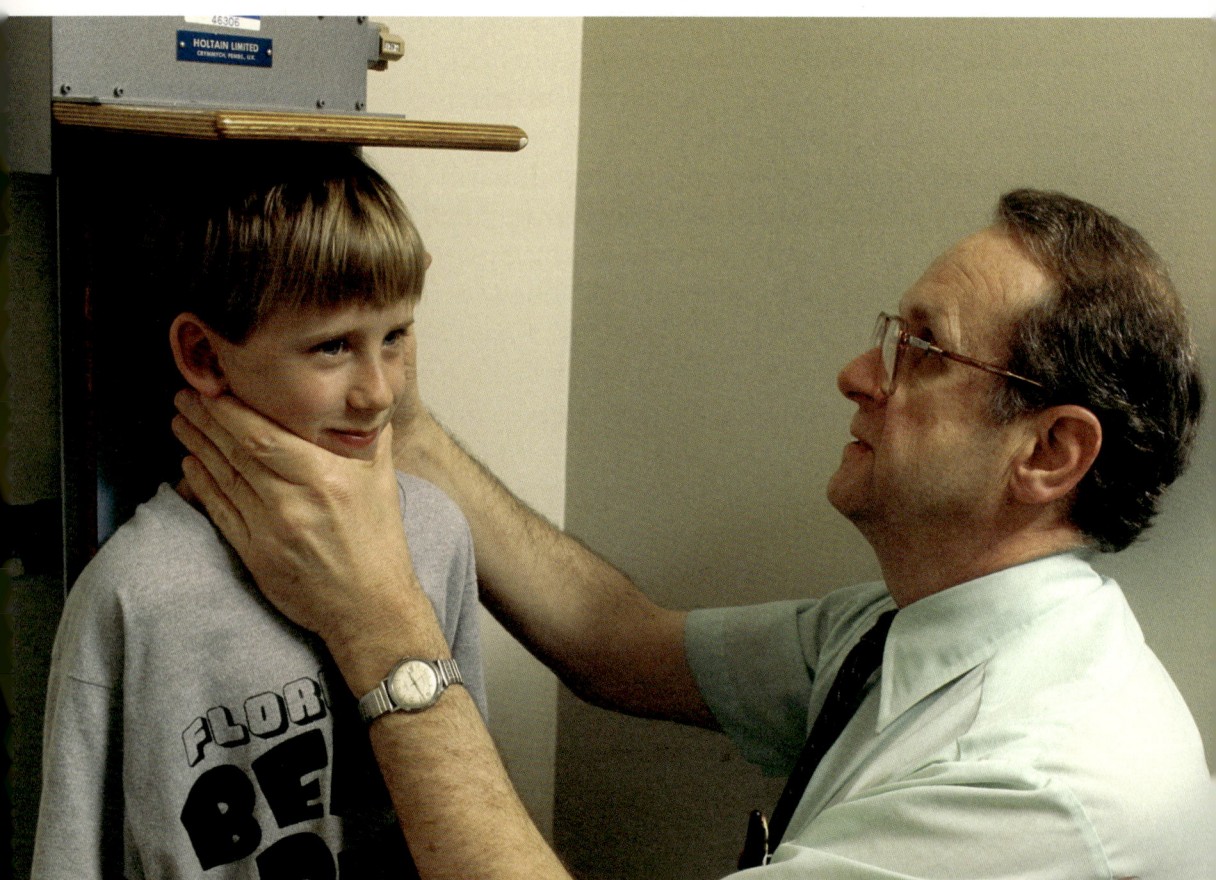

Even children genetically destined to be short—and who are not deficient in growth hormone—can, with growth hormone treatments, gain up to four inches in height, depending on when the treatment begins. (Will & Deni McIntyre/Photo Researchers, Inc.)

The authors reported that discontinuing growth hormone therapy in adolescence would limit the child's ability to attain "peak bone mass." They suggested that "growth hormone should be administered in adequate doses and for an adequate length of time to help achieve a bone mineral density within normal range."

Another potential benefit of continuing treatment throughout adolescence is the effect of growth hormone on a child's later risk of developing heart disease. In addition to the increase in total body fat and abdominal fat associated with the hormone deficiency, blood levels of low-density-lipoprotein cholesterol (LDL, the so-called bad cholesterol) and triglycerides tend to be abnormally high. Because there is evidence that abnormal lipid levels in early adulthood raise the risk of cardiovascular disease in middle age or later, the *Pediatrics* authors suggest continuing hormone therapy throughout adolescence.

Are There Risks?

As Dr. Gordon noted, the long-term effects of growth hormone therapy are not known, particularly for children whose hormone levels are normal to begin with. There has been some concern that IGF-1, a protein produced by the liver that mediates the action of growth hormone, may raise the risk of developing cancer. When the hormone is administered, IGF-1 levels rise.

Dr. Ross said that "we monitor the levels of IGF-1 in children treated with growth hormone and adjust the dose so that IGF-1 stays within normal range." Thus far, she said, there has been no evidence of an increased risk of cancer recurrence in children with leukemia who were treated with growth hormone, although there has been a slight increase in recurrence in children with brain tumors.

VIEWPOINT 2

Human Growth Hormone Recipients May Be at Risk for Adrenal Crisis

National Endocrine and Metabolic Diseases Information Service

Natural pituitary human growth hormone was banned in the 1980s after a few people using it to treat their growth hormone deficiency died of Creutzfeldt-Jakob disease (CJD), a degenerative brain disorder. Recent studies, however, have revealed an even greater threat to those who have been treated with pituitary growth hormone: adrenal crisis. Some people who lacked growth hormone also lack ACTH, a pituitary hormone that directs the adrenal gland to make cortisol. Cortisol is necessary for life, especially during times of physical stress, injury, or illness. A lack of cortisol can lead to a fatal adrenal crisis unless it is recognized and promptly treated with medication. Growth hormone therapy itself does not cause adrenal crisis, but those receiving treatment for GH deficiency should be aware of the symptoms and danger signs of having too little cortisol, the author warns. This selection is excerpted from a health alert provided by the National Endocrine and Metabolic Diseases Information Service, an educational arm of the National Institute of Diabetes and Digestive and Kidney Diseases, one of the National Institutes of Health.

SOURCE: National Endocrine and Metabolic Diseases Information Service, "Health Alert: Adrenal Crisis Cause of Death in Some People Who Were Treated with hGH," National Institutes of Health (NIH), September 2010.

Doctors conducting the follow-up study of individuals treated with hGH [human growth hormone] looked at causes of death among recipients and found some disturbing news. Many more people have died from a treatable condition called adrenal crisis than from CJD [Creutzfeldt-Jakob disease]. This risk does not affect every recipient. It can affect those who lack other hormones in addition to growth hormone.... Death from adrenal crisis can be prevented.

Adrenal crisis is a serious condition that can cause death in people who lack the pituitary hormone ACTH. ACTH is responsible for regulating the adrenal gland. Often, people are unaware that they lack this hormone and therefore do not know about their risk of adrenal crisis.

Who Is at Risk?

Most people who were treated with hGH did not make enough of their own growth hormone. Some of them lacked growth hormone because they had birth defects, tumors or other diseases that cause the pituitary gland to malfunction or shut down. People with those problems frequently lack other key hormones made by the pituitary gland, such as ACTH, which directs the adrenal gland to make cortisol, a hormone necessary for life. Having too little cortisol can be fatal if not properly treated.

Treatment with hGH does not cause adrenal crisis, but because a number of people lacking growth hormone also lack ACTH, adrenal crisis has occurred in some people who were treated with hGH....

- *Why should people treated with hGH know about adrenal crisis?* Among the people who received hGH, those who had birth defects, tumors, and other diseases affecting the brain lacked hGH and often, other hormones made by the pituitary gland. A shortage of the hormones that regulate the adrenal glands can

FAST FACT

The primary function of the adrenal glands is to prepare the body for "fight or flight" when faced with threatening or stressful circumstances.

Growth Disorders

cause many health problems. It can also lead to death from adrenal crisis. This tragedy can be prevented.

- *What are adrenal hormones?* The pituitary gland makes many hormones, including growth hormone and ACTH, a hormone which signals the adrenal glands to make cortisol, a hormone needed for life. If the adrenal gland doesn't make enough cortisol, replacement medications must be taken. The most common medicines used for cortisol replacement are:
  - Hydrocortisone
  - Prednisone
  - Dexamethasone

What Is Adrenal Crisis?

Adrenal hormones are needed for life. The system that pumps blood through the body cannot work during times of physical stress, such as illness or injury, if there is a severe lack of cortisol (or its replacement). People who lack cortisol must take their cortisol replacement medication on a regular basis, and when they are sick or injured, they must take extra cortisol replacement to prevent adrenal crisis. When there is not enough cortisol, adrenal crisis can occur and may rapidly lead to death.

- *What are the symptoms of lack of adrenal hormones?* If you don't have enough cortisol or its replacement, you may have some of these problems:
  - feeling weak
  - feeling tired all the time
  - feeling sick to your stomach
  - vomiting
  - no appetite
  - weight loss

When someone with adrenal gland problems has weakness, nausea, or vomiting, that person needs immediate emergency treatment to prevent adrenal crisis and possible death.

- *Why are adrenal hormones so important?* Cortisol (or its replacement) helps the body respond to stress from infection, injury, or surgery. The normal adrenal gland responds to serious illness by making up to 10 times more cortisol than it usually makes. It automatically makes as much as the body needs. If you are taking a cortisol replacement drug because your body cannot make these hormones, you must increase the cortisol replacement drugs during times of illness, injury, or surgery. Some people make enough cortisol for times when they feel well, but not enough to meet greater needs when they are ill or injured. Those people might not need cortisol replacement every day but may need to take cortisol replacement medication when their body is under stress. Adrenal crisis is extremely serious and can cause death if not treated promptly. . . .

Symptoms occurring in individuals who are lacking in adrenal hormones include weakness, constant fatigue, lack of appetite, vomiting, and weight loss. (© Max Paris/Alamy)

Treating Adrenal Crisis

People with adrenal crisis need immediate treatment. *Any delay can cause death.* When people with adrenal crisis are vomiting or unconscious and cannot take medicine, the

Diagram of Endocrine Glands

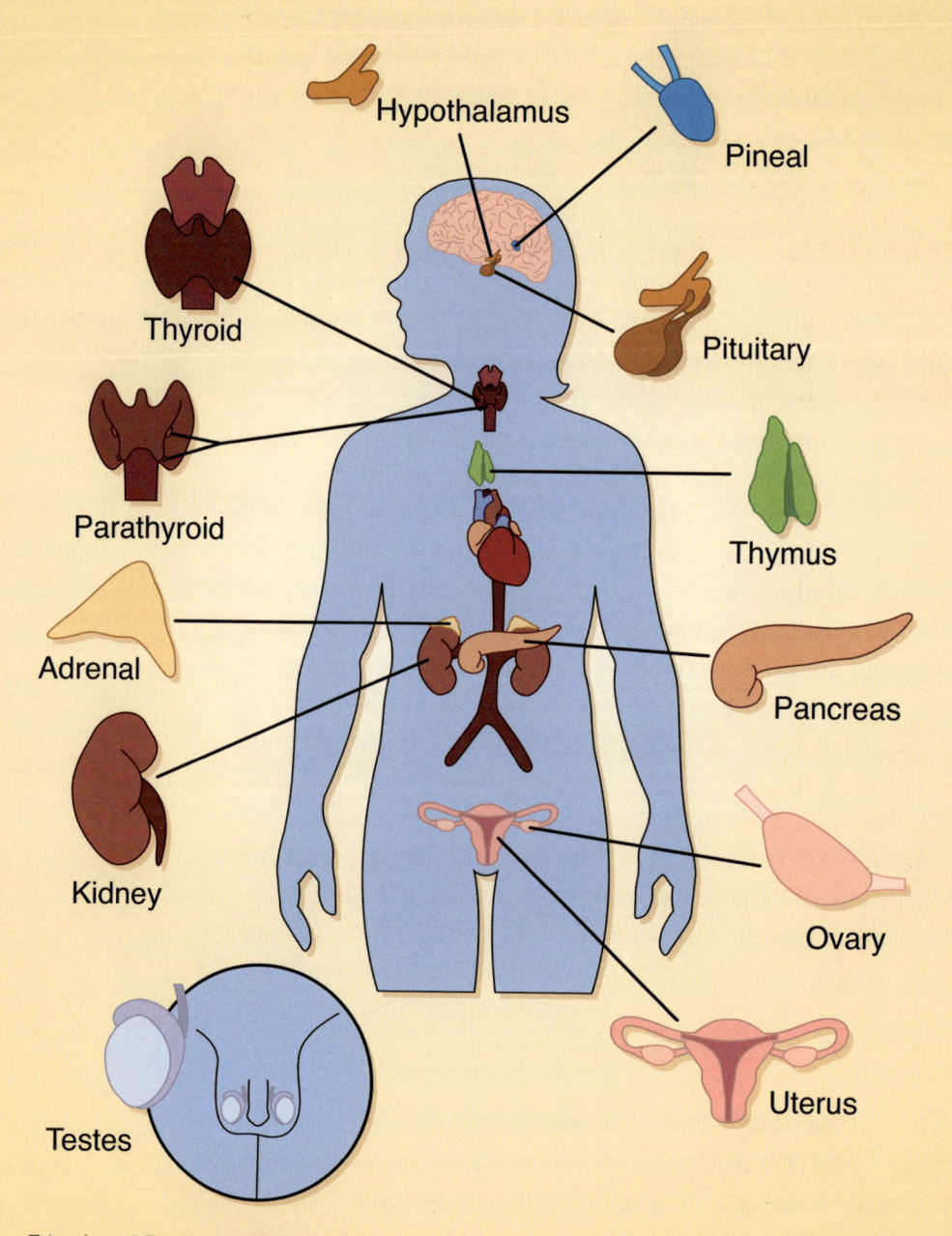

- Hypothalamus
- Pineal
- Thyroid
- Pituitary
- Parathyroid
- Thymus
- Adrenal
- Pancreas
- Kidney
- Ovary
- Testes
- Uterus

Taken from: © The Hormone Foundation.

hormones can be given as an injection. Getting an injection of adrenal hormones can save your life if you are in adrenal crisis. If you lack the ability to make cortisol naturally, you should carry a medical ID card and wear a Medic-Alert bracelet to tell emergency workers that you lack adrenal hormones and need treatment. This precaution can save your life if you are sick or injured.

- *How can I prevent adrenal crisis?*
  - If you are always tired, feel weak, and have lost weight, ask your doctor if you might have a shortage of adrenal hormones.
  - If you take hydrocortisone, prednisone, or dexamethasone, learn how to increase the dose when you become ill.
  - If you are very ill, especially if you are vomiting and cannot take pills, seek emergency medical care immediately. Make sure you have a hydrocortisone injection with you at all times, and make sure that you and those around you (in case you're not conscious) know how and when to administer the injection.
  - Carry a medical ID card and wear a bracelet telling emergency workers that you have adrenal insufficiency and need cortisol. This way, they can treat you right away if you are injured.

Remember: *Some people who lacked growth hormone may also lack cortisol, a hormone necessary for life. Lack of cortisol can cause adrenal crisis, a preventable condition that can cause death if treated improperly.* Deaths from adrenal crisis can be prevented if patients and their families recognize the condition and are careful to treat it right away. Adrenal crisis is a medical emergency. Know the symptoms and how to adjust your medication when you are ill. *Taking these precautions can save your life.*

VIEWPOINT 3

Early Puberty Is Linked to Environmental Toxins

Kim Ridley

Many American children are reaching puberty earlier than children of previous generations, writes Kim Ridley in the following selection. Known as "precocious puberty," this phenomenon manifests as physical signs of sexual maturity (e.g., pubic hair and breast development) before the age of nine. Some cases can be traced to children's accidental exposure to hormones in drug prescriptions, but a growing amount of evidence points to endocrine-disrupting chemicals as the source of the increase in cases of early puberty, the author points out. Endocrine disruptors and hormone-mimicking substances can be found in plastics, flame retardants, and pesticides. Dietary and lifestyle changes can reduce children's risk for precocious puberty, the author maintains.

Kim Ridley is a science writer and editor whose essays have appeared in the *Boston Globe*, the *Christian Science Monitor*, *Ode*, and other print and online venues.

SOURCE: Kim Ridley, "Raging Hormones," *Ode Magazine*, January–February 2007. Copyright © 2007 by Ode Magazine. All rights reserved. Reproduced by permission.

Kids these days are growing up too fast—in more ways than one. American girls are reaching puberty up to a year earlier than in previous generations, with some children showing signs of sexual development as young as age 3. In extreme cases, girls are budding breasts before they've even learned to read.

Researchers call this phenomenon "precocious puberty," which some say is on the rise. Forty-eight percent of African-American girls and 15 percent of Caucasian girls show physical signs of puberty by age 8, according to a study of 17,000 U.S. girls published in *Pediatrics* in 1997. In a subsequent study of more than 2,000 boys, lead author Marcia Herman-Giddens found that 38 percent of African-American boys and 30 percent of Caucasian boys showed signs of sexual development by age 8.

What's going on? Although scientists have yet to prove definitive causes, many suspect that hormone-mimicking chemicals, obesity and stress all contribute to precocious puberty. The chemicals, often called endocrine disruptors, are of particular concern because they're everywhere—in food, water, personal-care products, some plastics and many consumer goods.

Accidental Exposure to Hormones

Pediatrician Darshak Sanghavi notes in the *New York Times* (Oct. 17, 2006) that outbreaks of precocious puberty are most often traced to accidental exposure to drugs in hormone-laden products. He describes a case in which a kindergarten-age boy and his younger sister had both begun growing pubic hair. In addition, the boy was exhibiting aggressive behaviour.

When Sanghavi's colleagues examined the children, they discovered that both had extremely elevated levels of testosterone—equivalent to those of an adult male—and that their father was using a concentrated testosterone skin cream "for cosmetic and sexual purposes." The children had absorbed the testosterone from normal skin contact with their father.

It's a problem that's not likely to go away anytime soon. The *New York Times* notes that prescriptions for products containing testosterone are on the rise, doubling to more than 2.4 million between 2000 and 2004.

Endocrine Disruptors

Of course, we can't blame it all on testosterone. Phthalates, ubiquitous industrial plasticizers common in everything from personal-care products to vinyl and plastic packaging, mimic estrogen. So do compounds in some pesticides and flame retardants. A growing body of evidence suggests that these and other endocrine-disrupting chemicals can interfere with sexual development, an idea widely introduced in the groundbreaking book *Our Stolen Future* by Theo Colburn, Diane Dumanoski, and John Peterson Myers.

In the two decades since the book's publication, evidence has mounted that substantiates its main thesis. *Alternative Medicine* (Sept. 2006) points out that a number of human studies have found possible links between endocrine disrupters and early puberty. One study found that

Symptoms of Precocious Puberty

In girls, precocious puberty is when any of the following develop before age nine:	In boys, precocious puberty is when any of the following develop before age nine:
• Armpit or pubic hair	• Armpit or pubic hair
• Beginning to grow faster	• Growth of the testes and penis
• Breasts	• Facial hair, often first on the upper lip
• First period (menstruation)	• Muscle growth
• Mature outer genitals	• Voice change (deepening)

Taken from: National Center for Biotechnology Information and US National Library of Medicine, 2009.

Puerto Rican girls whose breasts developed earlier were three times more likely to have elevated levels of phthalate esters in their blood. Another reported that girls who had been accidentally exposed in the womb to polybrominated biphenyls—common flame retardants containing compounds that mimic estrogen—began menstruating a year earlier than a control group.

Some researchers have linked precocious puberty with factors including obesity, stress, and a sedentary lifestyle. "In the animal industry, to hasten puberty, they keep the animals confined, they feed them really rich diets, and they grow really fast," Marcia Herman-Giddens notes in *Alternative Medicine*. "That is exactly what we are doing to our children."

> **FAST FACT**
>
> According to pediatrics specialist Alan Greene, precocious puberty is ten times more common in girls than in boys.

Psychological Trauma

As young children struggle to cope with changing bodies, the psychological trauma can lead to later problems including depression, substance abuse and teenage pregnancies, according to a number of studies. Meanwhile, parents wrestle with painful decisions such as whether or not to give their children injections of drugs like Lupron, an expensive medication that suppresses hormones and has some 26 possible side effects.

Dr. Paul Kaplowitz, chief of endocrinology at Children's National Medical Center in Washington, D.C., and author of *Early Puberty in Girls: The Essential Guide to Coping with this Common Problem*, distinguishes between actual precocious puberty and more benign and isolated signs such as body odour, pubic-hair growth or breast development before recommending treatment, according to *Alternative Medicine*. He notes that less than 10 percent of the girls referred to him require treatment for early puberty.

Parents can take steps to minimize their children's risk of early puberty by encouraging healthy lifestyle choices, including the avoidance of meat, milk, and dairy products that contain growth hormones, as well as minimizing the use of soy. (© Age fotostock/SuperStock)

Still, what's happening now in children's bodies affects their daily lives and their future health—and may well foreshadow broader environmental and social crises.

Preventive Measures

Parents can take practical steps to minimize their children's risk for early puberty and encourage healthy lifestyles. These are key steps according to Sherrill Sellman, author of *What Women Must Know to Protect Their Daughters from Breast Cancer*:

- Avoid meat, milk and dairy products containing growth hormones;
- Buy organic produce;
- Minimize soy, which mimics estrogen;

- Choose green household products;
- Encourage children to eat well and exercise;
- Prevent children from chewing on plastic toys;
- Avoid polyvinyl chloride (PVC) products, including vinyl shower curtains and toys and packaging that bear the number "3," indicating they're made with PVC.

Schedule an appointment with a health-care practitioner, Sellman says, if your child shows unusually early signs of puberty. In addition, since phthalates are rarely included on cosmetics labels, visit sites like www.safecosmetics.org to find the safest personal-care products. Many of these small steps can help reduce your child's exposure to endocrine-disrupting chemicals while cumulatively contributing to a healthier planet. And that bodes well for all children.

VIEWPOINT 4

Early Puberty Is Linked to Obesity

Joanna Dolgoff

Joanna Dolgoff, a pediatrician specializing in child and adolescent weight management, is the author of *Red Light, Green Light, Eat Right*. In the selection that follows, Dolgoff argues that the increase in cases of early-onset puberty is a result of the childhood obesity epidemic. Because fat tissue is metabolically active and able to produce hormones like estrogen, children who are overweight are more likely to enter puberty early, she points out. Currently, there is no conclusive data proving that exposure to environmental chemicals speeds up puberty. Dolgoff maintains that early-onset puberty can lead to other medical problems, and she urges parents to get help for their children if they are overweight.

A new study from the journal *Pediatrics* finds that girls are beginning to develop breasts at the early age of 7 or 8. These results support the findings of a 1997 study that noted puberty beginning in girls at the

SOURCE: Joanna Dolgoff, "Obesity, Early Puberty—Leads to Health Problems," basilandspice.com, August 16, 2010. Copyright © 2010 by Joanna Dolgoff. All rights reserved. Reproduced by permission.

age of 7 or 8. But why are our children starting puberty so much earlier? Evidence indicates that the increasing rates of obesity play a major role.

The Connection Between Fat and Puberty

According to current medical understanding, puberty normally begins in girls between ages 8 and 12 and in boys between ages 9 and 14. Historically, "precocious puberty" (early-onset puberty) has been defined as before the age of 8 for a girl and before the age of 9 for a boy. The beginning of puberty is marked by penile enlargement or pubic hair growth for boys and breast bud formation and pubic hair growth for girls. If a child shows such signs of puberty before this age, she is sent to a pediatric endocrinologist for a full workup.

Why does obesity lead to early-onset puberty? Adipose (fat) tissue is metabolically active; fat tissue produces estrogen. The more fat tissue a child has, the more estrogen she is exposed to. It is generally accepted that overweight kids begin puberty earlier for this reason.

The presence of increased amounts of environment chemicals that mimic the effects of the sex hormones may also speed up the onset of puberty. To date, there is no evidence to prove that assumption. Dr. Frank M. Biro, the author of this new study, believes environmental chemicals are playing a role and will begin studying girls' hormone levels and lab tests measuring their exposures to various chemicals. More research needs to be done before we can conclusively state that these chemicals are affecting our children.

Health Challenges

Early-onset puberty can lead to medical problems. Girls who begin menstruating early have a slightly increased risk of breast cancer than other girls; such girls have a longer lifetime exposure to estrogen and progesterone,

Prevalence of Obesity Among Boys Aged 12–19 Years, by Race/Ethnicity United States, 1988–1994 and 2007–2008

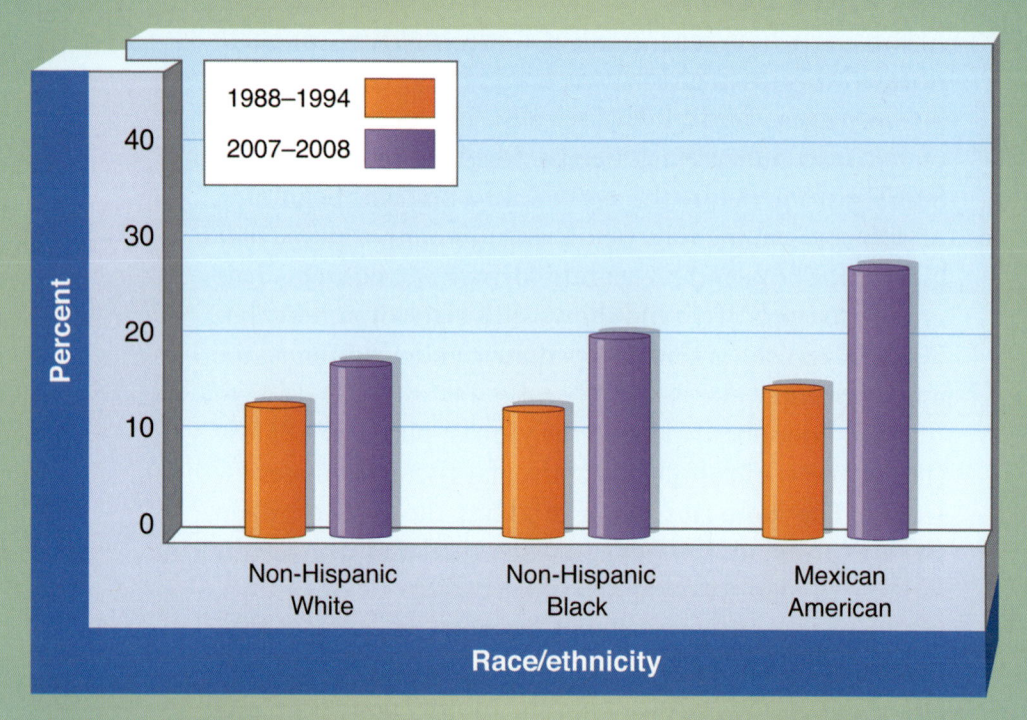

Taken from: CDC/NCHS National Health and Nutrition Examination Survey (NHANES), 1988–1994 and NHANES 2007–2008.

which can increase the growth of certain tumors. While this study looked at breast growth and not menstruation, breast growth is also a sign of hormone exposure and likely also indicates an increased risk of cancer.

Kids with early-onset puberty also suffer from short stature. While they initially appear taller than their peers, their growth plates close early, preventing the attainment of normal height. The child who was the tallest in her class soon becomes shorter than her friends.

Issues and Controversies Surrounding Growth Disorders

Girls with early puberty are also more likely to have polycystic ovarian syndrome (PCOS). PCOS is a hormone disorder that begins in puberty and causes infertility, acne, and other endocrine abnormalities.

Racial Differences

The onset of puberty differs among races. African American and Hispanic children often begin puberty earlier than kids of other races, even when weight is taken into account. This differential was confirmed in the current study. While all kids seemed to enter puberty earlier, African American and Hispanic children began the earliest.

When adipose (fat) tissue is metabolically active, the tissues produce the hormone estrogen. It is generally believed that overweight kids begin puberty earlier for this reason. (© Catchlight Visual Services/Alamy)

Growth Disorders

Not all doctors agree with the results of this study. Dr. Catherine Gordon, a pediatric endocrinologist and specialist in adolescent medicine at Children's Hospital Boston, said that so far, most evidence showed that neither breast development nor menstrual age had changed for white girls of normal weight. Yet according to Dr. Biro, "our analysis shows clearly that the white participants entered puberty earlier than we anticipated."

> **FAST FACT**
>
> The National Youth Risk Behavior Survey reported in 2009 that 12 percent of US high school students were obese.

The new study included 1,239 girls ages 6 to 8 who were recruited from schools and examined at one of three sites: the Mount Sinai School of Medicine in Manhattan, Cincinnati Children's Hospital or Kaiser Permanente Northern California/University of California, San Francisco. The group was roughly 30 percent each white, black and Hispanic, and about 5 percent Asian.

At 7 years, 10.4 percent of white, 23.4 percent of black and 14.9 percent of Hispanic girls had enough breast development to be considered at the onset of puberty.

At age 8, the figures were 18.3 percent in whites, 42.9 percent in blacks and 30.9 percent in Hispanics. The percentages for blacks and whites were even higher than those found by the 1997 study that was one of the first to suggest that puberty was occurring earlier in girls.

The New Norm?

The question remains, when should doctors refer a child for a precocious puberty workup? Some endocrinologists worry that if we accept puberty beginning at age 7 or 8 we would overlook serious medical problems, like endocrine diseases and tumors. On the other hand, if this earlier puberty is the new norm, why should we frighten families and waste valuable time and money on unnecessary tests? At this time, current practice does warrant a workup for any girl who shows signs of puberty before age 8.

It is clear that early-onset puberty is just one more effect of the child obesity epidemic. It is imperative that we help our overweight children attain a healthy weight as soon as possible. Parents are urged to get help for their overweight kids as soon as they begin to show signs of abnormal weight gain.

Little People Are Demeaned in Popular Culture

Lynn Harris

People with dwarfism are frequently portrayed in negative and degrading ways in popular culture, argues Lynn Harris in the following article. One advocacy and support group, Little People of America (LPA), confronts prejudice by filing complaints against advertisers and the entertainment industry when they reinforce mocking attitudes toward people with dwarfism. LPA also hopes to educate the public about the word *midget*, which is today considered an offensive way to describe a person of very short stature. Harris notes that the community of little people is divided about whether actors who play fantasy roles (such as elves or leprechauns) in television and film are perpetuating undignified stereotypes. But most members of LPA agree that social discrimination against people with dwarfism must be challenged.

Award-winning journalist Lynn Harris has written articles for the *New York Times*, *Glamour*, and other publications.

SOURCE: Lynn Harris, "Who You Calling a 'Midget'?," Salon.com, July 16, 2009. This article first appeared in Salon.com at http://www.salon.com. An online version remains in the Salon archives. Reprinted with permission.

Jimmy and Darlene Korpai of Crawford, N.Y., will always remember the night they fired Donald Trump's "Celebrity Apprentice."

It was this past April [2009], and the contestants' task was to create a viral video promoting All detergent.

"I got a bad feeling as soon as I heard them say 'small and mighty,'" says Jimmy, referring to All's line of highly concentrated soaps.

His instincts were dead on. "What about if we use little people and let them wash themselves in All detergent in the bathtub . . . and you hang them out to dry?" suggested superstar running back Herschel Walker. Joan Rivers: "We can hang them out on my terrace."

The resulting video, starring motorcycle maven Jesse James and titled "Jesse James Gets Dirty With Midgets," features three very short actors clad in All-bottle blue, whose yelling and hose-squirting and zippy fast-motion action (including an unexplained mallet to James' gut) leave his T-shirt sparkling clean.

"Imagine if I said what Herschel Walker did about a black person," says Jimmy, 37, a sculptor and designer. But it wasn't that, or the video, or the peppering of the episode with the word "midget," which—as even some on the show noted—is considered derogatory by people with dwarfism, that left the Korpais truly aghast. More than anything, it was this assurance, made to the group by James: "[Little people] know that people point and laugh at them and they are comfortable within themselves and they have fun right back."

"Here is a celebrity," Jimmy says, "telling people that it's all right to point and laugh at our daughter."

The Korpais are the parents of Hailey, 3, who has achondroplasia, the most common form of dwarfism. (The standard definition of dwarfism includes anyone 4-foot-10 or smaller whose stature is attributed to one of at least 200 medical conditions that cause dwarfism.)

Growth Disorders

Little People of America

Like approximately 80 percent of parents of children with dwarfism, Jimmy and Darlene are of average stature. Their efforts to educate—and reassure—themselves about Hailey's condition brought them to their local chapter of Little People of America, a 5,000-member organization offering medical information, social support and, increasingly, community outreach and political advocacy for dwarfs and their families. (Past and present agenda items: outlaw "dwarf tossing," lower the height of ATMs, raise awareness about advances in genetics—or, depending on one's view, eugenics.) The Korpais soon found themselves determined to help alter the culture into which Hailey had been born, which, for all its advances in civility—when was the last time you heard somebody called "a cripple"?—still finds "midgets" fair game for ridicule. The two have spearheaded an effort on the part of LPA to file a formal complaint about "Celebrity Apprentice" with the FCC [Federal Communications Commission]. Says Darlene, 36, who raises Hailey full-time: "In this p.c. [politically correct] world, I don't see why we're the last group it's OK to make fun of."

Which brings us to right now—and to what dwarfism expert and LPA stalwart Dr. Betty M. Adelson calls a "historic moment" for people with profound short stature. (Note: Adelson is my mother-in-law; my sister-in-law, Anna, 34, has achondroplasia.)

Dwarfs have weathered "Under the Rainbow" and the Oompa Loompas and approximately 158 sightings of "the plane, the plane"—not to mention Howard Stern's "Eric the Midget" and Pedro Martinez's "lucky" one: roles and gags in which the whole point, and source of matter-of-taste hilarity, is that the guy is, you know, *really short*. That's not going away soon.

Progress

But there's been progress. In "The Station Agent," actor Peter Dinklage played a fully realized leading character

The acting talent of the versatile Peter Dinklage has smashed the stereotypical view that little people are suited only to playing leprechauns and Oompa-Loompas. **(Robert Pitts/Landov)**

who was, you know, also short. LPA considered Fox's "The Littlest Groom" "equal-opportunity embarrassment" for all involved; plus, hey, lots of people loved Charla on "The Amazing Race."

Today, the best-known, most-visible dwarfs on TV are not blue-suited scrubbing bubbles but members of the Roloff family, whose real lives are chronicled—sensitively and in-depth, by most accounts—on one of TLC's [The Learning Channel's] most popular shows, "Little People, Big World." (There's also "The Little Couple," and the frequently aired one-off "Little Parents, Big Pregnancy," both of which are doing well.)

That's "historic" on its own. But the dwarfism community itself, insofar as it's represented by LPA, has also been transformed. Back in the day, Adelson says, "dwarfs kept very busy trying to show they were like everyone else." Not so with the "new generation": media- and Internet-savvy dwarfs and their parents, like the Korpais, who grew up watching other disability and rights groups form their identities and stake their claims. So now, more than ever before, LPA is coming out swinging.

PERSPECTIVES ON DISEASES AND DISORDERS

Proactive Steps

The group has recently taken two proactive and unprecedented steps: disinviting the Radio City Christmas Spectacular's "elf" recruiters from LPA's annual national conference, held last week [early July, 2009] in Brooklyn, N.Y.—and announcing at the conference, officially, and once and for all, that the word "midget" is anathema.

"When referring to people of short stature, Little People of America will use the terms 'dwarf,' 'little person,' 'person with dwarfism,' or 'person of short stature,'" reads the group's statement. "In addition to promoting positive language around people of short stature, Little People of America will . . . spread awareness to prevent use of the word 'midget,' considered offensive by Little People of America."

I attended the conference as a reporter. Over and over, the participants I interviewed—including one black mother of a toddler with achondroplasia—made the same analogy: The "M-word" should be considered as unacceptable as the "N-word."

Perhaps now you're reminded of the "R-word": that is, last summer's clamorous—and controversial—protest of the use of the word "retard" in the movie "Tropic Thunder." Then and now with the LPA, it has been incorrectly reported that advocates have demanded an all-out "ban" on the word in question. (That wouldn't fly with the FCC, anyway, whose policing of content is actually pretty limited, and which doesn't expressly ban words at all—not even the so-called seven dirty ones.) The stated goal of both campaigns: open eyes, boost sensitivity, get folks to think twice.

Ousting the M-Word

But—snarkosphere notwithstanding—there's reason to believe that the M-word campaign might be welcomed a bit more graciously outside the disability community than was its predecessor. While many of us embrace and defend "retard" and "retarded" as pungent synonyms for "dumbass," many also use the word "midget" as simple description. "Many people don't realize the word 'midget' is offensive in the first place," says Gary Arnold, 38, vice-president of public relations for LPA (and public relations coordinator for a disability rights and service group in Chicago).

People, that is, like the Gray Lady [the *New York Times*] herself. A March [2009] article buried in the *Times*' business section mentioned, in passing, a famous photo showing "J. P. Morgan Jr. with a midget who had been plopped in his lap by an opportunistic publicist." Outcry from dwarfs and their families—including detailed historical background provided by Adelson, author of two authoritative books about dwarfism—had this notable result: a rare addition to the *New York Times*' style manual. (Changes are made only five or six times a year, according to a spokesperson.) As public editor Clark Hoyt wrote in April, the new entry states that people of unusually (and medically) short stature should be referred to as dwarfs, not "midgets."

Still, LPA's ousting of Radio City and its anti-"midget" campaign are—like the history and usage of the word itself—not without complication or controversy.

Etymologically, at least, it's easy to explain the word's offense: It's derived from "midge," a type of tiny fly that may bite or spread disease. But part of the word "midget's" P.R. problem is that the term (like "retarded") was once used comfortably, particularly to distinguish people who were small but proportionate (usually as the result of a growth hormone deficiency) from those who were small but disproportionate (usually due to one of various bone disorders, such as achondroplasia). It was also once the term of choice for dwarfs in the entertainment world. In fact, LPA itself was founded in 1957 by actor Billy Barty and about 20 colleagues as "Midgets of America." The

Growth Disorders

name was changed three years later. Even, or especially, as more diverse (and "respectable") professions have opened up to people with dwarfism, its vestigial freak-show connotation has remained, and has come to rankle.

Would people with dwarfism ever seek to sap the word's power by reclaiming it, as the gay rights movement has done with "fag" and "queer"? Some think it's way too soon; some think it's way too hurtful. Says Adelson: "I don't think they'll ever want it back."

What About "Dwarf"?

What about the word "dwarf"? Given its association with "gnome," "elf"—and, you know, Dopey, Grumpy and Sleepy—it's not everyone's first choice. (Barbara Spiegel, 35, of South Portland, Maine, has achondroplasia and two young daughters, one adopted, with the same diagnosis. Recently the elder, Alexandra, asked how she should describe herself to her new kindergarten classmates this fall. "You can say you're a dwarf," replied Spiegel. Alexandra: "But I'm not make-believe!") Still, since "dwarf" is an accurate term for a medical diagnosis, it's not considered offensive, at least in the United States.

Not everyone is a fan of "little person," either, which to some sounds mythical and munchkin-y. On the upside—as Billy Barty himself was said to point out—the term does contain the word "person." According to Adelson, the acronym "LP" (often used by members of LPA in place of "little people") is the neologism of choice in the U.S., precisely because it carries so little historical baggage. ("Most individuals," she adds, "prefer simply to be called by their given names.")

Even if LPs *could* ban the word "midget"—or find the perfect term to describe themselves—neither mockery nor bias ... would magically vanish overnight. What would *really* help stop the laughing and pointing at the "midget" on the street? Advocates within LPA agree: the understanding that people with dwarfism are actual humans, not mythical creatures or comic relief. It's an understanding, they say, that can come in large part from seeing dwarfs portrayed realistically and respectfully in pop culture.

"Whenever we look at the progress we're making, or trying to make, we can assign credit—or blame—to images of dwarfs in culture and media," says Gary Arnold.

To Be or Not to Be—an Elf

That's where Santa's dancing elves come in—and that's where things get complicated again. The decision to uninvite Radio City after nobody-even-knows-how-many years was made by 2009's New York conference organizers alone, not by LPA as a whole. The planners for the 2010 gathering in Nashville fully intend to have Radio City's elf recruiters return.

Ask the first group, and they'll acknowledge that many LPs (often amateurs with unrelated career aspirations) enjoy performing in the show, and stress that those who are interested should by all means seek out the opportunity on their own. But LPA, they say, should not appear to endorse or place its imprimatur on an enterprise that can be seen as perpetuating age-old dwarf stereotypes. (And, as one parent of a dwarf wondered: "How will parents at their first LPA conference feel if it looks like this is the only opportunity that awaits their child?")

Nashville organizers feel otherwise. "My daughter did Radio City and she loved it," says conference organizer Sheryl Hankins, who is of average stature. "She's a pediatric oncology nurse. At no point in her life did she think she had to be an elf to make a living. I think other people realize dwarfs are not just elves, too. I guess I just give everyone more credit than that."

Former "elves" are divided as well. My sister-in-law performed in Radio City's Chicago show one year, and now wishes she hadn't. But for actor Mark Povinelli, 37, who is well under 4 feet tall, it was different (possibly, in part, *because* he's an actor). "I mean, part of me was like, ugh, I can't believe I'm doing this—but every actor says that at some point," he says. Plus, he notes, the generous salary is what helped him afford to go on to do Shakespeare and Durang in the months that followed.

The Challenges of Short-Statured Actors

Even those opposed to Radio City's presence at the conference—or, more broadly, who are bothered by the limited roles available to dwarfs—stop far short of condemning the actors who choose to play those roles.

"When people with dwarfism are portrayed negatively, they are usually portrayed *by* people with dwarfism," observes Joe Stramondo, 27, chair of LPA's advocacy committee and a doctoral candidate in bioethics at Michigan State University. "This complicates the issue."

Few actors of any height are in the position to cherry-pick plum roles, if you will. Most, in fact, can rarely afford to say no. Given how often roles come along like Dinklage's in "The Station Agent," this leaves many very-short-statured actors to choose, in effect, between supporting their families or playing Jimmy Kimmel's left testicle.

"When I first get a script, I flip through to see where I'm going to bite someone's ankle or punch someone in the nethers or fight the tall guy," says Povinelli. (Povinelli will admit, with a sheepish smile, that early in his career he did in fact play Kimmel's testicle. It should be noted that he went on to play [famed French painter Henri] Toulouse-Lautrec—a role normally performed by an average-statured actor on his knees—at Lincoln Center and tour many countries as Torvald Helmer of Lee Breuer's "Dollhouse," a modern version of the Ibsen drama.)

That said, there's no simple formula for determining which roles are "negative" in the first place. For one thing, it's not necessarily as simple as highbrow vs. lowbrow. (We're talking to you, Gary Oldman.) Povinelli also says that, perhaps counterintuitively, it's often the "fantasy" roles (leprechauns, goblins, denizens of the HarryPotter-verse) that offer more depth than the real-guy ones.

"Some people give LPs a hard time about the costumed fantastical characters they play, but in fact, that's some of the most meaningful, meaty work we have available," he says. Cases in point: On "Charmed," he played a leprechaun warrior with an interesting story line and complex motivations. On "Dharma and Greg," he played Greg's old college roommate, who was . . . short. (All the ensuing short jokes made "inadvertently" by a rattled Dharma were supposed to be at her expense. But they were still . . . short jokes.)

Povinelli agrees that the word "midget"—and all it conveys, on-screen and off—is an issue to be addressed. "But what bothers me most is being invisible," says Povinelli. "People butting in front of me because they think I'm a child, or being hit in the head with carry-on bags. The other day I was at the supermarket, pushing a full cart, the handle way up there, and in front of me there was a woman reaching down to the bottom shelf to get something. I didn't see her, and totally plowed into her, knocked her down. It gave me the weirdest sensation: I loved it. That had happened to me, in some way, so many times, and now *I* was the asshole doing it. It gave me some sort of sick satisfaction," he says. "You can call me 'midget'—that's your problem, not mine. But when you ignore me as a human, when you don't give me the courtesy you'd give a person of average height, that's when it really gets me."

> **FAST FACT**
>
> The Little People of America was founded by renowned dwarf actor Billy Barty. Other actors with dwarfism include Kenny Baker (R2-D2 in the *Star Wars* movies), Zelda Rubenstein (the psychic in *Poltergeist*), Verne Troyer (Mini-Me in the *Austin Powers* movies), and Hervé Villechaize (Tattoo on *Fantasy Island*).

Acceptance of Dwarfism Is Preferable to Surgery

Dan Kennedy

Dan Kennedy is a writer, blogger, commentator, and assistant professor of journalism at Northeastern University in Boston, Massachusetts. He is also the father of a child with dwarfism. In the commentary that follows, Kennedy questions the cultural perception of dwarfism as a disability and argues that limb-lengthening surgery is unnecessary and potentially dangerous. He maintains that dwarfs are not people who are broken and in need of fixing; rather, it is society's attitudes about dwarfism that need to change. It is important to recognize that people with dwarfism are ordinary people who deserve acceptance just the way they are, Kennedy concludes.

One morning last week, I spent an hour talking about dwarfism with 50 or so fourth-graders at a private school in the Boston suburbs. They had just finished reading Lisa Graff's *The Thing About Georgie*, a charming novel about a dwarf boy trying to come to

SOURCE: Dan Kennedy, "A Little Reality," *The Guardian*, December 2, 2008. Copyright © 2008 by The Guardian. All rights reserved. Reproduced by permission.

terms with his identity. One of their teachers recalled that I'd written a book about raising our daughter, Becky, who, like Georgie, has achondroplasia, the most common form of dwarfism.

The kids' questions were smart and direct. How does Becky reach the light switches? Will she be able to drive? Does she go to a regular school? Do people stare? Somehow, though, it didn't occur to any of them to ask whether Becky would choose to be taller if she could. Perhaps that was because Graff's depiction of Georgie is so well-rounded —tough, honest and matter-of-fact. As with Becky, being a dwarf is just a part of who Georgie is. Who would want to change such a thing?

Dwarfism in the Media

Which brings me to the latest depiction of dwarfism by the news media. This past Sunday [November 30, 2008], the *Washington Post Magazine* published a story about a

Three Forms of Disproportionate Dwarfism and Their Symptoms

Achondroplasia	Hypochondropasia	Spondyloepiphyseal Dysplasia Congenita
• average size-trunk • disproportionately short arms, legs, fingers • particularly short upper arms and upper legs • large head • bowed legs • swayed lower back • limited mobility at elbows average adult is 4 feet tall	• average size-trunk • disproportionately short arms, legs, fingers • broad, short hands & feet • limited mobility at elbows • symptoms similar to achondroplasia but less pronounced • Average adult is 5 feet tall	• short trunk • short arms, legs, neck • average-size hands and feet • feet are twisted ("clubfoot") • hunching curvature of upper spine • swayed lower back • vision and hearing problems • average adult is 3 to 4 feet tall

Taken from: Mayoclinic.com, August 27, 2009, and Genetics Home Reference, June 2006.

Growth Disorders

teenage girl with dwarfism named Caitlin Schroeder, who's undergone dangerous, painful surgery to add nearly six inches to her height. The story, written by Caitlin Gibson and photographed by Rebecca Drobis, is extraordinarily well-done, sensitive, thorough and full of nuance. The *Post* deserves considerable praise.

Yet, at more than 8,000 words, illustrated by 15 pictures, the package may be the most extensive look at dwarfism ever provided by the *Post*, or, for that matter, any major American newspaper. And it is, at root, dedicated to the proposition that dwarfism is wrong, and is something to be changed.

Back in August 2002, I spent some time with Caitlin Schroeder's surgeon, Dr. Dror Paley, making the rounds with him at Sinai Hospital in Baltimore and interviewing him afterwards at a nondescript Middle Eastern restaurant tucked inside a strip mall. I also interviewed Paley's best-known patient, Gillian Mueller, then 27, the first American with dwarfism to undergo the procedure. (My book, *Little People*, is now out of print, but the full text is online.)

Mueller had come through her ordeal beautifully. At nearly five-foot-two, you would not know that she was a dwarf; the only giveaways were her small hands and slightly awkward gait. But elongated limb-lengthening, or ELL, as it is called, is gruesome business. The bones of the legs and arms are broken, and metal pins mounted to cylindrical frames are inserted from the outside. The patient turns the pins to separate the bones by about a millimeter a day. Though Caitlin Schroeder opted to stop at a little less than six inches, dwarfs can, and have, added a foot or more to their height.

It can be dangerous, too—infections and nerve damage are not uncommon. Death is a possibility. Paley is a gifted, experienced surgeon. But as Dr. Michael Ain, an orthopedic surgeon at Johns Hopkins Hospital who has achondroplasia, told me, "The complication rate is incredibly high. They've gotten better, but it's still amazingly high." Why take the risk?

Why Fix People Who Are Not Broken?
The reason is that despite the lip service we pay to diversity, we all have a vision of the perfect child, and are willing to do whatever it takes to make that vision a reality. No one wants to be the parent whose kid gets stared at, pointed at, laughed at. I'm not necessarily talking about Caitlin Schroeder and her family, whose reasons seem sound and well-thought-out; I've got a broader cultural critique in mind.

"Our society is designed for easier accessibility around the height of about five feet tall, maybe even taller than that," Paley told me six years ago, talking about door knobs, gas-pump handles, even coat hangers as reasons to consider major, life-altering surgery.

He was right, at least from inside his own view of reality. But in talking about dwarfism as a socially constructed disability, Paley left no room for the possibility that society could change—is changing, for that matter—

This bone-lengthening implant contains a telescopic nail (lower center) that is implanted in the human tibia (above). Once implanted, the nail is extended by about one millimeter a day over several months to induce new bone growth. (Pasquale Sorrentino/ Photo Researchers, Inc.)

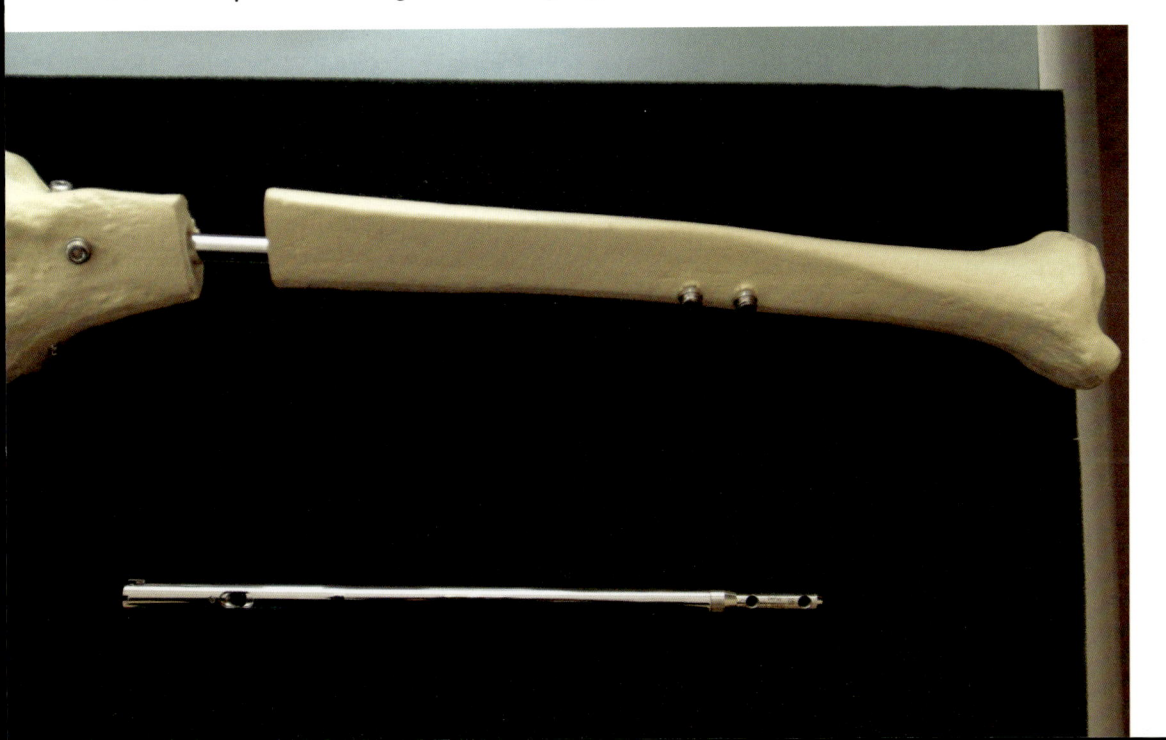

Growth Disorders

and that, ultimately, that's better for all of us than attempting to fix people who aren't broken.

We are under no illusions about the challenges Becky faces. She's four-foot-one, and, at 16-years-old, is about as tall as she's going to get. Her arms are disproportionately short. She waddles. But though her genome is imperfect, she, Becky, is perfect just the way she is.

> **FAST FACT**
>
> The advocacy group Little People of America has taken an official stand against limb-lengthening surgery, warning of the risks of long-term nerve and vascular damage.

For us, and for her, stools, pedal-extenders for driving and healthy self-esteem are far superior to months of surgery and agonising rehab, not to mention the uncertain prospects for a good outcome. The one time we showed Becky a television news story about limb-lengthening, she was fascinated, but she made it clear that she wanted nothing to do with it.

Then again, unlike Caitlin Schroeder, Becky has been exposed to people with dwarfism, adults and kids, from the time she was a toddler, and she knows first-hand the good lives they lead. To Becky, Matt and Amy Roloff are not the stars of the reality show *Little People, Big World*—they're ordinary people with whom she had her picture taken some years back, when Matt was president of Little People of America and we were attending the annual conference.

As impressive as the *Post*'s story is, what's missing is the sense of dwarfism as another type of normal. Maybe we're not there as a culture—yet. But we're moving in that direction. Little by little, you might say.

Numerous Complications Are Associated with Limb-Lengthening Procedures

Little People of America Medical Advisory Board

The following selection is a position statement composed by the medical advisory board of Little People of America (LPA), a support and advocacy organization for people with dwarfism and other people of short stature. The board maintains that extended limb-lengthening (ELL) surgery is performed mainly for cosmetic and social reasons rather than for medical necessity, and the board warns that the procedure can lead to several serious complications. It encourages prospective ELL patients to carefully consider all their options by undergoing evaluations before surgery, including a risks-and-benefits analysis, orthopedic and vascular assessments, and psychological counseling.

The following position summary is not intended to either advocate for or condemn extended limb lengthening. It is meant to be a measured summary of information that may be of value to members of the

SOURCE: Little People of America Medical Advisory Board, "Extended Limb Lengthening Position Summary," 2006. Copyright © 2006 by Little People of America. All rights reserved. Reproduced by permission.

Growth Disorders

Extended limb-lengthening (ELL) is effective in preventing certain orthopedic and neurological complications. However, the procedure is often performed now for adaptive, cosmetic, and psychosocial reasons. (© doc-stock/Alamy)

small stature community and members of Little People of America.

The techniques for leg lengthening were originally developed for correction of limb length discrepancy and are an accepted therapy for this. Over the past two decades the procedure has been expanded to allow for symmetric lengthening in individuals of short stature. Although this newer application has generated widespread interest, it has also created controversy among both medical [professionals] and persons of short stature and their families.

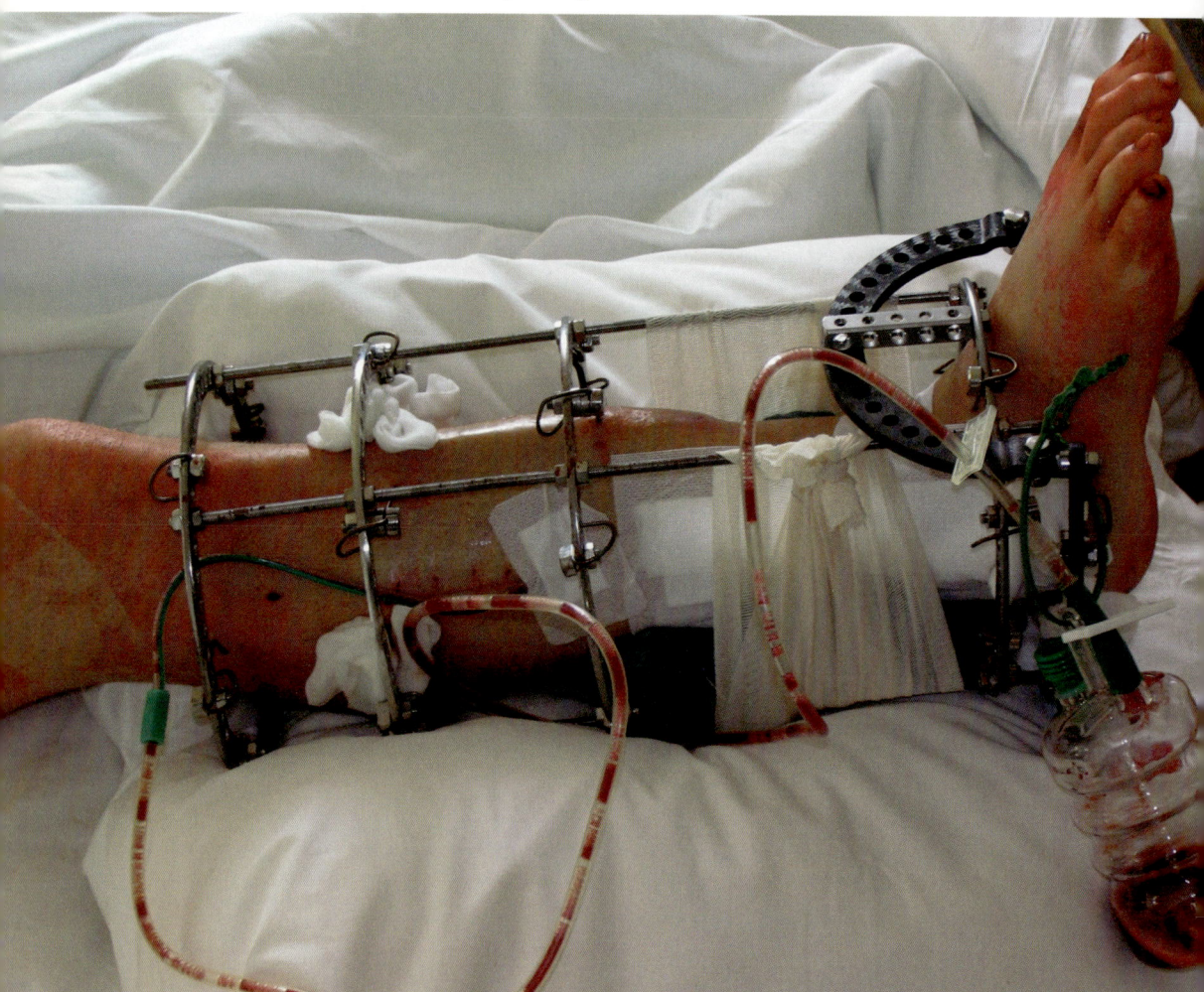

There are no established medical indications for symmetric extended limb lengthening (ELL). While it may have benefit in preventing certain orthopedic and neurological complications in some skeletal dysplasias, the procedure is primarily being performed for adaptive, cosmetic, and psychosocial reasons.

Research is being done on the safety and long-term functional outcome of this procedure. Currently no prospective, randomized studies have yet been completed.

Potential Complications

The possible complications of ELL are numerous. These include:
- Nerve injury (usually temporary);
- Infection;
- Angulation;
- Non-union;
- Increased contractures (of the hip, knee and/or ankle);
- Fractures;
- Unequal limb lengths;
- Increased risk for late onset osteoarthritis.

Although the acute complication rate associated with ELL has been reduced, it is still substantial.

This is what patients should have prior to initiation of ELL:
- Confirmation of a specific short-stature diagnosis. The relative risks and benefits of ELL are different in different types of skeletal dysplasias.
- Counseling concerning the natural history and genetic implications of the relevant skeletal dysplasia, independent of ELL.
- Adequate discussion of the benefits and risks of ELL (including medical complications, financial issues, educational and psychological concerns).

Prospective patients should be of an age to participate fully in these discussions and in the decision-making process.

Growth Disorders

Necessary Evaluations

We recommend that before, during and after ELL operative procedures, evaluation should include:
- Orthopedic assessment;
- Physical therapy assessment, including evaluation of mobility, activity, functional limitations, etc.;
- Clinical neurological evaluation;
- Peripheral vascular assessment;
- Psychological evaluation, including self-image, body image, peer relationships, and family relationships.

All of these evaluations will require the cooperative involvement of orthopedic surgeons, physical and occupational therapists, medical geneticists, radiologists, psychologists and/or psychiatrists, and social workers in

What Is Osteoarthritis?

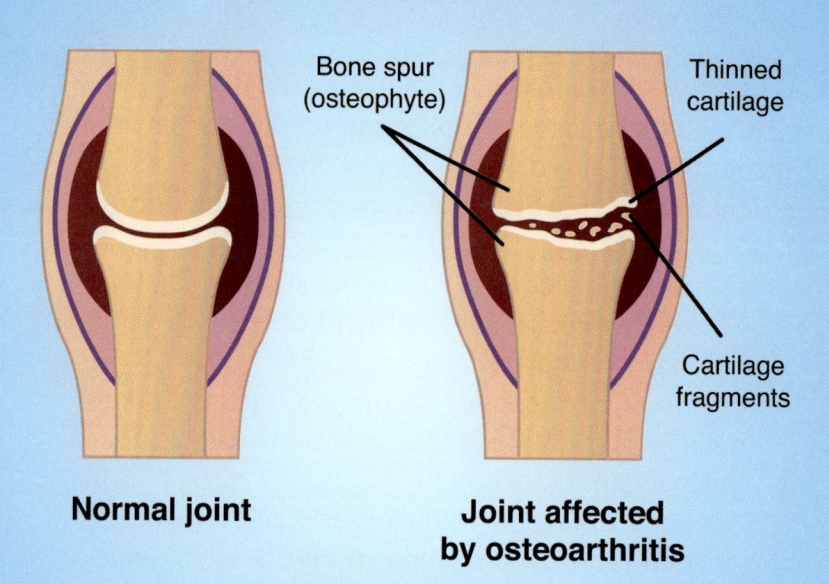

Normal joint — Joint affected by osteoarthritis

Bone spur (osteophyte); Thinned cartilage; Cartilage fragments

Taken from: Doctor Exclusive.com, February 13, 2011. http://doctorexclusive.com/?p=3261.

Issues and Controversies Surrounding Growth Disorders

longitudinal management. We caution prospective patients and their families to seek out institutions that offer the broad multidisciplinary approach that is needed. An institution should have a program with special emphasis and expertise in skeletal dysplasia. The institution should be equipped to follow the patient for a decade or more.

Complete success of ELL is not guaranteed. Furthermore, ELL will not change other health-related needs of individuals of short stature. They will still need to have ongoing care by someone knowledgeable about the natural history of their specific diagnosis.

ELL is a complex procedure with far-reaching implications. Interested individuals should carefully assess the institution and personnel, as well as all risks and benefits of ELL prior to committing to this procedure.

> **FAST FACT**
>
> According to Short Persons Support, people who undergo cosmetic limb-lengthening procedures face a 25 percent chance of complications after the surgery.

VIEWPOINT 8

Genetic Research May Lead to the Prevention of Dwarfism

Phil Sneiderman

The following selection is excerpted from a Johns Hopkins University press release that reports that Kalina Hristova, an expert in the field of membrane biophysics, is conducting cutting-edge research on how a defective protein produced by a genetic mutation causes achondroplasia, a common form of dwarfism. Her approach is unusual in that she is using physics and engineering approaches—rather than biological experiments—to analyze how the defective protein interacts with a cell membrane. If Hristova can determine how the cell membrane is influenced by this protein, researchers will be closer to finding a way to treat or prevent dwarfism.

Achondroplasia, a common form of dwarfism, is caused by a genetic mutation: A single incorrect building block in a strand of DNA produces a defective protein that disrupts normal growth. If a scientist

SOURCE: Phil Sneiderman, "Materials Scientist Seeks Dwarfism Clues in a Cell's Membrane," Johns Hopkins University, August 19, 2010. Copyright ©2010 by Phil Sneiderman. All rights reserved. Reproduced by permission.

Issues and Controversies Surrounding Growth Disorders

could figure out precisely how this errant protein causes trouble, then a way to avert this chain of events might be found.

Sounds like a job for a biologist. Or maybe not. The person who cracks this mutation mystery might just be a Johns Hopkins engineer who works with cell membranes.

Kalina Hristova, an associate professor of materials science and engineering, has spent more than five years in a nontraditional effort to understand how that tiny DNA error leads to dwarfism. Hristova, an expert in the field of membrane biophysics, has focused her research on the thin protective covering that surrounds human cells, the plasma membrane; for this project, she is studying the activity of proteins that reside in this membrane. Among these proteins is the one linked to dwarfism.

Achondroplasia is the most common form of short-limbed dwarfism, occurring worldwide in fifteen thousand to forty thousand newborns each year. (Rick Wilking/Reuters/Landov)

Examining a Rogue Protein

A biologist might attack this puzzle by growing cells in a dish or conducting experiments with lab animals. Hristova, supported by a federal stimulus grant, instead has been using engineering tactics to determine how the protein may be wreaking havoc. Her lab has developed new tools and techniques that allow her to take pictures and make measurements that reveal how the rogue protein is behaving in the cell membrane. Her team's goal is to generate exact numbers that will yield clues about how the protein causes the cells to take a wrong turn.

"Unlike the biologists, we are not investigating what will happen to the cell in 20 days," she said. "We are looking at the initial events occurring in the cell membrane, the way proteins first interact there. As engineers, we have to strip down the system and simplify it so that we can see how it works. We are looking at the physics not the biology."

For her project, called "Seeking the Physical Basis of Achondroplasia," Hristova has received a $27,000 federal stimulus grant for lab equipment, which supplements her five-year grant of approximately $1 million from the National Institutes of Health [NIH]. Her award is among the 424 stimulus-funded research grants and supplements totaling more than $200 million that Johns Hopkins has garnered since Congress passed the American Recovery and Reinvestment Act of 2009, bestowing the NIH and the National Science Foundation with $12.4 billion in extra money to underwrite research grants by September 2010.

Searching for Causes

Achondroplasia, the focus of Hristova's grant, is the most common form of short-limbed dwarfism, occurring in one in 15,000 to 40,000 newborns (worldwide), according to the National Institutes of Health. The condition results from a mutated FGFR3 gene. In some cases, this mutation is passed down by at least one parent. But about 80 percent of those with achondroplasia have average-size parents and develop the condition because a new mutation occurs. This defective gene produces proteins that send "stop" signals, halting the growth of cartilage that makes room for normal-size long bones of the arms and legs.

Hristova cautions that no "cure" for achondroplasia exists and that her research is unlikely to produce one in the near future. She describes her work as basic research that could lay the groundwork for future treatment or prevention of achondroplasia. "Finding the cause of this condition is a very hard problem because the first thing you need to do is to understand what's happening at the molecular level, what these proteins are actually doing," she said. "Before you can solve a problem, you need to know what's causing it."

"Don't mind Ashley. After looking through a microscope all day, anything large startles him."

ScienceCartoonsPLUS.com

Growth Disorders

The proteins Hristova is examining are tiny threads of amino acids embedded in the cell membrane, with one end extending inside the cell and the other wriggling outside. This arrangement allows the protein to gather information outside the cell and send messages to the nucleus, or control center, inside the cell. These messages provide instructions to the cell, including telling it whether or not to grow.

To find out how this process goes awry in people with dwarfism, Hristova is investigating how the mutated protein is embedded within the membrane, compared to the proteins of people who grow normally. Does one type stick farther inside or outside the cell? She also is trying to determine whether the growth disorder is related to the chemical and mechanical ways that the mutated proteins "talk" to other proteins in the cell membrane.

"Tricking" the Cells

To conduct these studies, Hristova and her team coax cells into making the protein, then "trick" the cells into giving up their membranes with the proteins still embedded in the material. The researchers then use a confocal microscope to gather information about the mutated proteins in these membrane segments without the constant turnover of molecules that occurs in an intact living cell. Her team also works with National Institute of Standards and Technology scientists in using a technology called neutron diffraction to collect images that show where the proteins are situated with respect to the membrane's surface. "We are using materials science techniques to conduct innovative research into why this form of dwarfism is occurring," Hristova said.

Hristova, whose parents are scientists, said that her entry into the field of membrane biophysics occurred

> **FAST FACT**
>
> Biophysicists study how physics, such as electrical and mechanical energy, relates to living cells and organisms.

"sort of by chance." In her native Bulgaria, while earning her undergraduate and master's degrees in physics, she became interested in biophysics. At one point, an instructor assigned her work on membranes, and she quickly embraced this area of research.

She came to the United States to pursue a doctorate in engineering and materials science at Duke, and then further honed her research skills as a postdoctoral fellow at UC [University of California at] Irvine. In 2001, she joined the faculty of the Whiting School of Engineering at Johns Hopkins, where she specializes in membrane biophysics and biomolecular materials and is an affiliate of the Institute for NanoBioTechnology. In 2007, Hristova received the Biophysical Society's Margaret Oakley Dayhoff Award for "her extraordinary and outstanding scientific achievements in biophysics research."

Her interest in the dwarfism mutation originated years ago when a physician talked to her about the problem and sparked her interest in finding a solution through engineering techniques. In recent years she has presented her findings at scientific conferences attended mainly by researchers who continue to study the disorder with the tools of a biologist. "Eventually, sometime in the future, both approaches will come together as we work toward a basic understanding of what causes achondroplasia," Hristova said. "Then someone will come up with a treatment."

CHAPTER 3
Living with Growth Disorders

VIEWPOINT 1

A Mother with Marfan Syndrome Discusses Her Decision to Have Children

Lucy Hunter

In the following selection, Lucy Hunter, a resident of Great Britain, discusses the challenges she faced upon discovering that she had passed Marfan syndrome on to her two sons. Lucy decided against genetic screening during her pregnancies, believing it would be wrong to abort a fetus with a manageable health condition. Still, she experienced some guilt when she realized her children would be living with the disorder, knowing from her own experience that they would encounter criticism and social rejection. She seeks ways to boost her sons' self-esteem, letting them know that their medical condition need not keep them from realizing their hopes and dreams.

Two days after my son Rufus was born, I knew for sure. It was during one of those interminable cups of tea, and chit-chat about breastfeeding. My baby boy nestled in the crook of my arm. The trainee midwife

Photo on facing page. People with growth disorders must often employ ingenuity to adapt to their environment. Here, for example, an individual unable to reach a container of milk solves the problem by climbing into the cooler. (Rick Wilking/Reuters/Landov)

SOURCE: Lucy Hunter, "The Long and Short of It: Marfan Syndrome," *The Independent*, March 18, 2008, p. 8. Copyright © 2008 by The Independent. All rights reserved. Reproduced by permission.

craned forward to get a closer look. "Ooh," she cooed brightly. "Hasn't he got long fingers?"

At which point I burst into tears. Not so unusual for a new mum, but this wasn't straightforward baby blues. The midwife confirmed what I already instinctively knew—I had passed on the genetic disorder Marfan syndrome to my baby.

Marfan syndrome is an inherited connective tissue disorder, which sufferers have 50 per cent chance of passing on. The gene that makes the protein fibrillin, and gives skin and connective tissue its stretchy feel, is faulty. Because connective tissue is found throughout the body, Marfan syndrome can affect the skeleton, eyes, heart and blood vessels, nervous system, skin and lungs. People with Marfan's tend to be unusually tall and slender, with particularly long arms, legs and fingers. Resulting heart problems, which include aortic dissection, can be deadly. For those undiagnosed and untreated, the average age of death is 32.

The outlook is much better for those diagnosed with the syndrome: 72. Nearly seven years on from giving birth, perspective has overtaken post-natal hormones, and I realise that our family is lucky. We are diagnosed and, thus far, are relatively mildly affected. Compared to other genetic disorders, it's manageable.

Living in the Shadow of Marfan's

It would be a mistake to see Marfan's as simply the sum of its medical parts. It affects looks as well as health. Apart from simply being gangly, those with Marfan's have less ability to store fat and muscle. I'm 5ft 11, and at 18 I weighed seven and a half stone [about 105 pounds]. Strangers presumed I was anorexic. What's more, people with Marfan's tire more easily, and feel like their bodies have let them down. Seventy-five per cent of sufferers inherit it, so many have experienced a parent who is in poor health, or has died prematurely.

Living with Growth Disorders

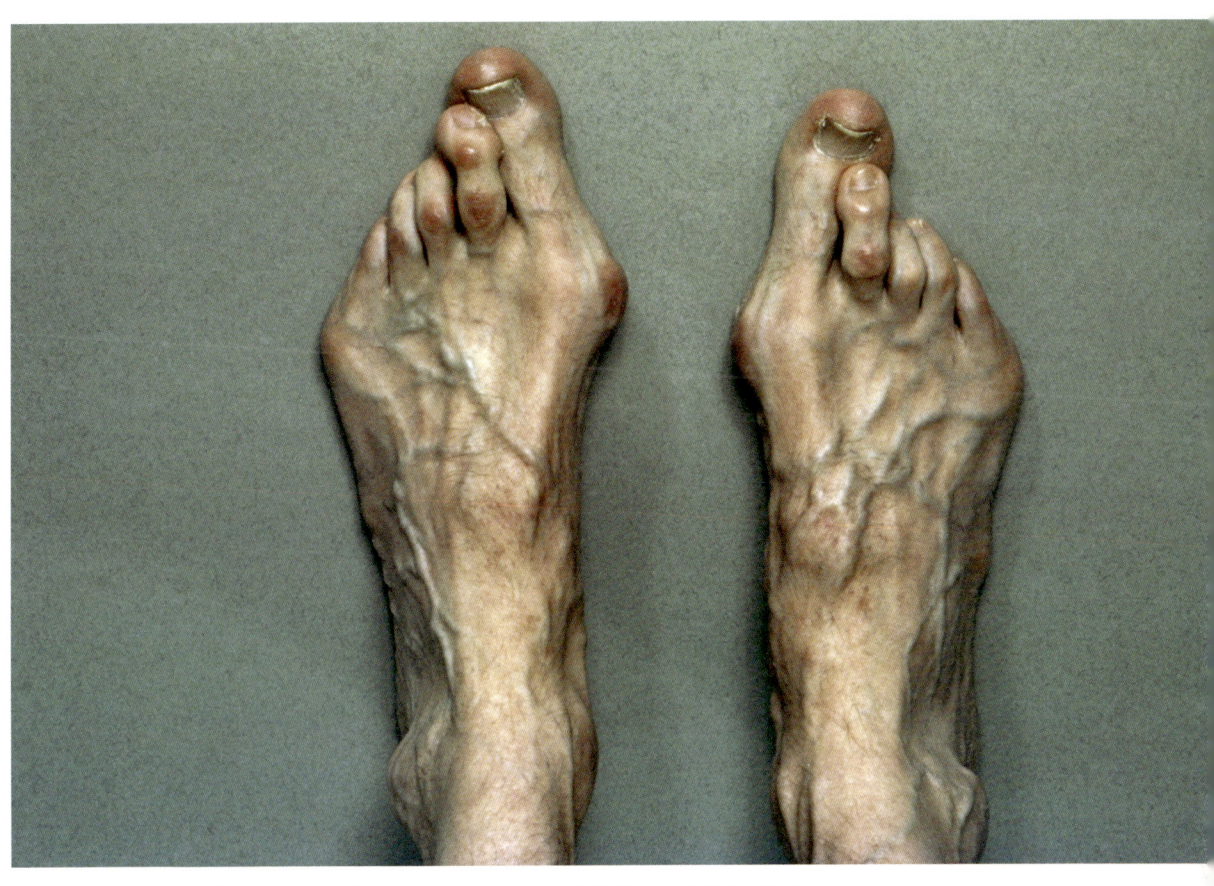

Marfan's cast a shadow over my childhood. My father was diagnosed in the late Sixties, and the knowledge that he was likely to die prematurely was a living grief. Perhaps unsurprisingly, he drank. He died in 1986, during an operation to replace his aortic valve. He was 52.

Taking a Chance on Nature

Throughout my twenties, I worried about passing on the gene to my children. Women with Marfan's are encouraged to have children by the age of 30. After genetic counselling, I considered the options. Although a prenatal test for Marfan's exists, the idea of aborting my own child because he is, well, like me, was absolutely abhorrent. I looked into the more palatable idea of having a "designer"

This photograph of the feet of a person suffering from Marfan syndrome shows abnormally elongated and slender toes. The syndrome is a genetic connective tissue disorder whose sufferers have a 50 percent chance of passing the gene on to their offspring.
(John Radcliffe Hospital/ Photo Researchers, Inc.)

PERSPECTIVES ON DISEASES AND DISORDERS

embryo implanted using IVF [in vitro fertilization]. Then I decided to take my chances on nature.

I have never regretted my decision, despite the guilt when I realised that Rufus, and Oisín, now four, had both been affected. More immediately, super-tall children bring their challenges. Rufus has always been taller than his peers, at one point wearing clothes up to four years older than his age. As a toddler he was a real handful—controlling regular-sized two-year-olds is hard, so you can imagine what it was like in our household.

ADHD [attention-deficit/hyperactivity disorder] and other learning disorders are more common in those with Marfan's, and Rufus shows some of these traits. Other parents, assuming he was much older, were openly critical over what was normal two-year-old behaviour. I got into the habit of sighing, "Oh, he's so tall for two—it's a real pain." A mistake—Rufus has absorbed the message that being tall is bad, damage I am trying to undo now.

Challenges with "Professionals"

When Rufus was three, he had a developmental check. Half an hour in, I realised that the doctor thought he was seven, as she hadn't read his notes. When I picked up on this, she was clearly embarrassed, and, as he was a few months short of four, said she was looking at the milestones for four. I was surprised. Teachers are usually very precise when they refer to the age of nursery children, because a month or two makes a big difference. When the doctor sent me her report, she had recorded that Rufus was four years and nine months, and based her findings on that.

Oisín, my younger son, has not experienced the same level of criticism from others—partly because he's not as tall as Rufus, and he has the savvy of a second child. So it was upsetting to receive a visit from the health visitor, who had assured me that she was knowledgeable about Marfan's. Oisín has the typically slender physique that is a hallmark of the condition. But the health visitor was horrified and demanded to know whether I fed him. I smiled tightly, assured her I did, and prayed I wouldn't be plunged into one of those nightmare stories when social workers storm in and sweep children into care.

Bullying and Self-Esteem

I can't be naive. The effects of Marfan's are going to become more marked as they progress through childhood. A news story two years ago [2006] made my blood run cold. A 13-year-old girl with Marfan's, Caroline Stillman, was bullied out of school after suffering vicious verbal abuse and physical harassment because she looked different. My father grew up in war-time Middlesbrough, a tough town for even the most robust, never mind for a red-headed, bespectacled boy with Marfan's. Strangers told him to "Eff off back to Auschwitz [a Nazi concentration camp]." By the Seventies, my sister Madeleine (who is also affected) and I had been told to Eff off back to Ethiopia [home of many starving children].

I am constantly looking for ways to bolster my boys' self-esteem. Oisín is a natural joker, and I think he'll be able to handle the jibes. Rufus is sensitive, and has already told me he hates being different. When the time comes to explain his birthright, I hope that he'll take some comfort from the fact that although Marfan's makes you different, it doesn't stop determination, talent and even genius.

Considering its rarity, Marfan's has more than its fair share in the hall of fame—especially musically. There's the composer Sir John Tavener, Sergei Rachmaninov, Niccoló Paganini, Joey Ramone and Jonathan Larson, the writer of [the hit musical] *Rent*. Others believed to have the condition include Abraham Lincoln, [Pharaoh] Tutankhamun and Mary, Queen of Scots. According to some sources,

> **FAST FACT**
>
> In the United States, Marfan syndrome affects one in five thousand to one in ten thousand people.

there's [terrorist leader] Osama Bin Laden, too. I might keep quiet about that one.

Marfan syndrome is an interesting disorder, not just medically. It's one that challenges our moral code. As religious leaders and politicians debate abortion on the grounds of "serious handicap", I'm wondering whether Marfan's fits this criterion. I suspect that for many people, it does. But why? Because we look different? Or has the idea of premature death become totally unacceptable to us? Passing on Marfan's is daunting, I know. But what I find more terrifying is the move towards a world where those with physical flaws and treatable illness are not allowed to be born. We may be creating a new world, but it certainly isn't a brave one.

VIEWPOINT 2

Little People Seek Tolerance

Janese Heavin

In the following selection, *Columbia (MO) Daily Tribune* staff writer Janese Heavin profiles Mark McGimsey, a man with dwarfism. Since the dwarf population in the United States is not numerous—about thirty thousand—negative or mocking pop-culture portrayals of dwarfs have a significant impact on the public's perception of little people, Heavin notes. McGimsey finds that there is "nothing funny" about living with dwarfism as he faces continuing health challenges and annoying stares from people of normal height.

Mark McGimsey got over the teasing at an early age, but the occasional stare still has the power to annoy him. At 47, McGimsey has more important things to think about: a wife and two children, but also the physical problems that accompany his dwarfism. And, frankly, there's nothing funny about his scoliosis,

SOURCE: Janese Heavin, "Little People Seek Tolerance: Dwarfism Isn't Funny, They Say," *Columbia Daily Tribune*, October 7, 2009. Copyright © 2009 by Columbia Daily Tribune. All rights reserved. Reproduced by permission.

Growth Disorders

pinched nerves, metal rods in his spine, multiple knee surgeries and the future operations he faces because of his stature.

But it seems some in American society still think it's acceptable to mock people with dwarfism. "We're one of the last social groups where it's still somwhat OK to make fun of based on who we are," said Gary Arnold, vice president of public relations for Little People of America. To counter that culture, Little People of America has declared [October 2009] the first Dwarfism Awareness Month. "The hope is, by raising awareness over a month and recognizing dwarfism, . . . to educate the community and further advance care for these patients," said Dan Hoernschemeyer, a University of Missouri doctor who has treated some 60 patients with dwarfism from Missouri and nearby states.

> **FAST FACT**
>
> In movies, dwarfs are sometimes belittled or treated like children simply because of their diminutive size.

An estimated 30,000 Americans live with some form of dwarfism, and about 80 percent of those, including McGimsey, were born to parents of normal stature. Because the population is small in number, Arnold said, negative media portrayals and activities such as "midget wrestling" and "midget bowling" have a more significant impact on little people than negative connotations within other minority groups. "Even in a big urban area, you're not going to have exposure" to dwarfism "in your day-to-day routine life," he said. "So opinion and experience is definitely shaped by what you see in pop culture."

Social Ridicule

He doesn't have to go back to the days of Tom Thumb, the famous 19th-century circus dwarf, to find examples of social ridicule. This year [2009], Republican National Committee Chairman Michael Steele, arguing the party needs to be more diverse, joked that they should include "one-armed midgets." And this spring, Little People of America filed a Federal Communications Commission complaint against the TV show "Celebrity Apprentice" and NBC for an episode that mocked little people.

At 4 feet 8 1/2 inches, McGimsey is tall for someone with dwarfism. The average height ranges from 2 feet 8 inches to 4 feet 5 inches, and the cutoff is 4 feet 10 inches. Although he doesn't require the footstools and extension tools many little people need to function in a tall world, his height has affected him. As a kid, McGimsey said, he wore a clumsy and painful back brace at night and faced constant taunting from peers. In college, he was known as the "hunchback" of the dorm. His wife, Jo Ann Grady, who is of normal height, had to adjust to the stares and whispers about their relationship. And when McGimsey tried to work in fish management, he fell into a stream with electrical rods and ended up getting shocked.

But he also tries to find the positive aspects. As a bat specialist for the Missouri Department of Conservation for three years, he found it easier to navigate caves than his taller colleagues did. Even becoming permanently disabled 10 years ago and having to give up the career he loved has a positive side. "The disability has allowed me to be a stay-at-home dad," he said, holding his 3-month-old daughter, Maeghan. "I had a great job, but it pales in comparison to being able to stay home with my children.... There's nothing better than a sleeping baby on your chest."

VIEWPOINT 3

Suffering Growth Hormone Deficiency as a Child

Anonymous

The following personal story is shared by a boy who recalls being teased at school for being short—even shorter than his younger sister. When medical tests revealed that he had a growth hormone (GH) deficiency, he learned that he would need daily shots of growth hormone in order to grow. There were times when he did not want to take the injections, but spurred by his mother's persistence, he continued with his therapy. This article was originally posted at the website of Major Aspects of Growth in Children, or the MAGIC Foundation, an organization dedicated to addressing children's growth issues.

I was short. My baby sister was taller than me. Kids at school picked on me and called me names—like shorty, shrimp and pee wee. It hurt my feelings and I know my mom and dad felt bad for me. My doctor sent us to a specialist to see why I was not growing and why I was so much smaller than my friends in school. The specialist said I

SOURCE: "Me and My Growth Hormone," magicfoundation.org, June 2, 2008. Copyright © 2008 by The Magic Foundation. All rights reserved. Reproduced by permission.

would have to take a test to check my growth hormone. My mom didn't know what growth hormone was. The specialist took a long time to explain it to her.

The day for the test came. I wasn't scared but I think my mom was. They did have to put an IV in my arm. It only pinched for a few seconds. The test took quite a few hours and I fell asleep for awhile. Before I knew it the test was over. But the specialist told my mom it would be 2 to 3 weeks before we would know how the test came out.

Daily Shots

The specialist called about 2 weeks later and told my mom to come back with me so they can tell us about the test results. They told us that I had growth hormone deficiency and would need to take growth hormone shots every day for me to grow. Boy did my mom have a lot of questions! I don't think she liked it when they told her that the parents give the shots. I wasn't scared so much. They said the shots would help me grow, and I wanted to grow, but my mom looked scared. I told her not to worry, it would be okay, but she even cried!

We went back to the specialist a couple of weeks later to get my growth hormone and for them to teach my

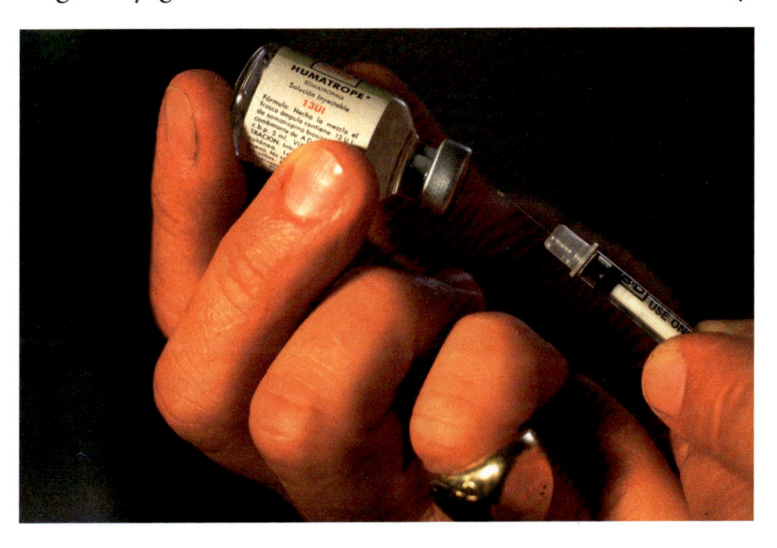

Individuals who receive treatment for growth disorders require daily injections of growth hormone until they stop growing.
(© Mark Downey/Alamy)

Growth Disorders

mom how to give the shots. I was a little scared even though they told me it was only a pinch. They were right—it was only a pinch! I think it hurt my mom because she thought I was scared. We went home ready to take my growth hormone shots. It took my mom awhile to get used to giving me the shots. Funny, she didn't seem scared any more after our first visit back to the specialist to find out I had grown almost 1 full inch. I guess this growth hormone really works!

New Clothes

Not too long after I started growing we had to get new shoes. My mom said it was the first time my feet grew in 2 years. Then my pants were above my ankles, so off to buy new pants too! Before growth hormone there were times I was sad, but after a few years of the shots I was catching up to other kids my age. They didn't call me names anymore and they let me play in all the games.

There were times I didn't want to take my shots. You know us kids can get stubborn at times! I was almost as tall as my friends, so why did I have to keep taking the shots? Well, my mom wouldn't listen. She had to make me understand that when I stopped taking the growth hormone shots I would also stop growing again. I guess she was right, so I didn't stop the shots.

I'm almost grown now. I'm in the normal range on a growth chart. Growth hormone is like a miracle drug to me. Back when I was six years old the specialist told my mom I was never going to be 4 feet tall without growth hormone shots. Today I'm 19 inches taller than I would have ever been, thanks to growth hormone! Was the testing, all the doctor visits, and all the shots worth it? You bet it was!!

> **FAST FACT**
>
> Insulin syringes used by diabetics are also used by growth hormone–deficient people to inject daily doses of human growth hormone because the needles are so thin they are nearly painless.

VIEWPOINT 4

The Impact of Turner Syndrome on a Young Woman

Collette

In the following selection, a British woman named Collette describes what it was like for her to grow up with Turner syndrome, a female chromosomal imbalance that, in most cases, results in short stature, an inability for puberty to occur normally, and infertility. Because Collette did not have access to growth hormone therapy (which is often used to treat Turner syndrome today), she remained short and has faced bullying and prejudice at school and at work because of her appearance. Collette also maintains that she received little sympathy and emotional support after her diagnosis. As a result, she has low self-esteem and feels very discouraged about her life.

I was diagnosed around 10–11 when my parents were worried that I was small for my age and pushed for investigations. I had a day of very unpleasant tests being on a drip which I hated at a Children's Hospital. I was told by my parents, a very much generational thing. My parents

SOURCE: "Turner Syndrome: Collette's Story," tellingstories.nhs.uk, 2006. Copyright © 2006 by University of Glamorgan. All rights reserved. Reproduced by permission.

Growth Disorders

Shown here is a light micrograph of the chromosomes of a woman with Turner syndrome. The disorder results from a missing or incomplete sex chromosome. (GJLP/Photo Researchers, Inc.)

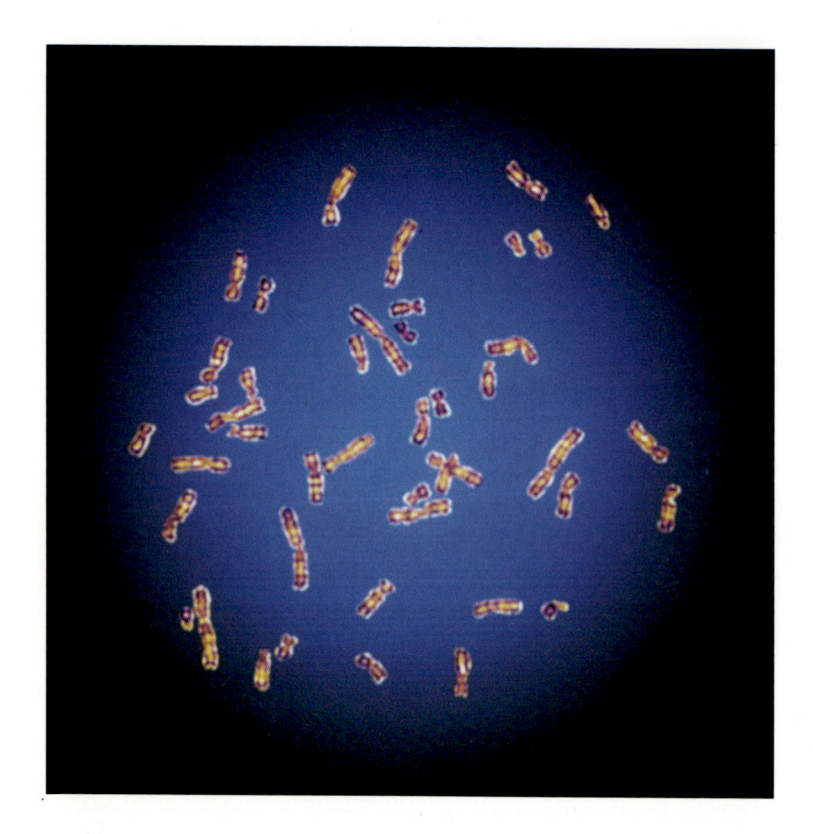

and I were told that I was going to be short and not have children. I was discharged to the care of my GP [physician] and that was it.

The Effect of Turner Syndrome on Everyday Life

I do believe that Turner's has affected my life and it does get me down. I have suffered bullying both at school and in the workplace. I am never going to achieve any potential that I might have because of my shape and size which is due to Turner's. I have a degree and I am doing a low grade clerical job within the Civil Service. If you do not fit the mould, you may as well forget it and I am not going to get the reports to allow me to get on and am at a disadvantage in the workplace because people will not, when it comes down to it, take me seriously or believe that I am capable of managing staff.

I feel that I am fighting a losing battle when it comes to walking in that interview room.

At 16, realising the meaning of the infertility issue was difficult. There was no one to talk to or give any support. I remember crying on a bus on the way home from a routine hospital visit. I was not allowed to grieve or be upset or hurt by my parents.

The Need for Support

To be put in touch with other TS Women in my home town and to have emotional support and help. Unless they are part of the TSSS [Turner Syndrome Support Society] they will not be known about. I can get on the phone but it is not the same as face to face. I would like clinics both paediatric and adult to put people in touch with each other. Parents may like to meet up and speak to someone who has the condition. When newly diagnosed clinics should be aware of the TSSS and give number etc. The book and DVD produced by the society should be available for parents to borrow from the clinic.

My generation had no TSSS to turn to and like every condition every generation benefits from more knowledge and better treatment. Growth hormone was not available and it would have helped to know that the difficulties that I had growing up with Math and Sports came from Turner's. My parents may have benefited too from the knowledge that is around today. There will [be] more developments that will allow even more girls to have their own families. My generation is the first one to benefit from IVF [in vitro fertilization]. I have been able to cope with IVF because it was either going to work or not.

I have been dealt with very clinically and very unsympathetically. They said she is going to be short and can't have kids and needs to take tablets for the rest of her life.

> **FAST FACT**
>
> The MAGIC Foundation reports that Turner syndrome patients benefit the most when growth hormone treatments start before age nine and estrogen therapy starts after age fourteen.

TS women do not feel like they are whole women because of what we lack. Boyfriends, if at all, come along much later. We do not get wolf whistles in the street or paid compliments on our appearance very often. What I would like to happen in clinics today for the girls is to have a sympathetic female ear to talk to other than their mum so that they can talk over issues that they may feel too embarrassed to bring up and discuss treatment with particularly during the teen years. They are the worst for TS Women and they need all the help they can get.

The Psychosocial Impact of Turner Syndrome

Later, Collette adds these reflections in relation to the discussion of the psychological impact of TS on her:

I feel that I have had everything taken away from me. Lack of fertility is very hard to live with and many TS women have to find fulfilment in other ways.

I thought at least with having a degree, I could look forward to some sort of career which would have helped.

Because of "The Curse of Turners"—looks and short stature and not being taken seriously, it is not going to happen.

Instead I have had to suffer bullying and lack of understanding, which has eaten away at any self-esteem I have had—lack of it is a common problem in TS and I have had to take sick leave (I am on my third bout now) because of it.

I am finding it very hard to cope.

VIEWPOINT 5

A Pro Wrestler with a Growth Disorder Talks About the Price of Fame

Kent Babb

The following piece by Kent Babb is a profile of wrestler Paul Wight, who worked for many years with World Wrestling Entertainment (WWE) where he was known as the Big Show and also as the Giant. Having grown up with an undiagnosed growth disorder, Wight was nearly seven feet tall by the time he finished high school. He underwent surgery to remove a pituitary gland tumor at age nineteen but gained a hundred pounds after the procedure, which ended his college basketball career. Winning a contract with WWE proved to be very lucrative for Wight, but his enlarged heart, five-hundred-plus-pound weight, and numerous muscle and joint injuries have also taken a toll on his health.

Kent Babb is a sportswriter who has written for the *Kansas City Star* in Missouri, and the *State*, a daily newspaper in Columbia, South Carolina.

SOURCE: Kent Babb, "The Large Price of Fame and Fortune: Aiken Co. Native with Growth Disorder Risked His Health," *The State*, June 17, 2007. Copyright © 2007 by The State Media Corporation. All rights reserved. Reproduced by permission.

Growth Disorders

There was a moment when the giant looked reborn. He moved with grace, bounced his fist off his opponent's skull, primed himself for victory.

What a way to go out it would be, to retire as world heavyweight champion. The Big Show is winning this wrestling match, pounding Bobby Lashley into oblivion. The only thing left is the Big Show's finishing move, the devastating....

Hold it. In a flash, Lashley flips the switch. Now he is pounding the Big Show. One... two... three punches and a running elbow that knocks the giant on his back. This is no way to go out—no way to begin the final descent of the Big Show's career, looking up at a snarling opponent.

Look around. Thousands have piled into James Brown Arena on this night, a Sunday in December. They came for this, to watch this main event and to watch the Big Show, who grew up less than an hour from the arena. In here, he is an attraction. Listed at 7 feet and 507 pounds, he is something to see. He is one of the largest characters in a business of tall tales.

Huge, Marketable—and Unhealthy

Out there, outside the ring and beyond the spotlights, he is Paul Wight. He grew up in New Holland, a town in rural Aiken County [South Carolina]. He was a football player and all-state basketball player at Batesburg's W.W. King Academy.

In here, he is marketable. His size has earned him millions of dollars, a house on a Florida lake and a diverse career as a wrestler, actor and businessman. Without his looming body, none of it would have been possible.

Out there, his size represents a health risk. Wight is morbidly obese and has an enlarged heart. His work and travel schedules allow little time for proper rest and nutrition, which has prevented many of his injuries from healing. He cannot stand for more than a few minutes. He cannot sit for much longer.

Living with Growth Disorders

Wight is 35 years old, but his mother, Dorothy, says her only son's body operates as if it were 40 years older.

Wight's size was partly caused by a tumor on his pituitary gland, which controls growth and tells most bodies to stop growing at a certain age. The tumor, which prevented those signals from reaching his brain, was removed when Wight was 19—and 7 feet tall—and nearly 350 pounds.

Was the tumor the best thing to happen to Wight or the worst thing? It created unimaginable opportunities. It also created a world of health problems that could shorten his life.

In here, none of that matters. He is the Big Show, and on this night that is what he is putting on. His job is to suspend reality, ignore its consequences and keep the thousands at James Brown Arena mesmerized by what might happen next.

But what comes next for Wight? As of this night, he has three months remaining on his contract with World Wrestling Entertainment [WWE]. His plans, according to Dorothy Wight, are to take time off and possibly retire. She and others have urged Paul Wight to stay retired, to stay out there for good.

But out there is reality. Out there, consequences are waiting.

One life offers riches and fame—at the expense of health. The other life stomps opportunities but promises a healthier, potentially longer life.

Even in a world of tall tales, straddling both sides can be done for only so long.

A Giant Upbringing

Dorothy Wight did the math and shook her head. The equation must have been off. Dorothy and her husband, Paul, did not notice their son's rapid growth until a Southern tradition yielded startling results.

The equation suggests that, at a child's first birthday, multiplying its height by three will predict its height as an

Growth Disorders

Professional wrestler Paul Wight, right, grew up with an undiagnosed growth disorder. (Jacob Langston/MCT/Landov)

adult. The result suggested the younger Wight would grow to 7 feet, 4 inches.

Dorothy, who is 5-foot-10, scoffed at the prediction. So did her 6-3 husband. Then again, Paul was always hungry. Two weeks after Paul's birth, Dorothy stopped buying baby formula because it served only as an appetizer. When she fried chicken, the baby smelled the cooking meat and screamed until his mother gave him a taste. Years later, when Paul was a teen, Dorothy needed a plan for her son's hunger, which required about 6,000 calories per day. Weekly trips to a wholesale food store yielded 10 pounds of ground beef and 50 pounds of potatoes.

"I was in labor for 14 1/2 hours," Dorothy says. "He didn't want to come out. When he was ready, he popped out, started growing and said he was ready to eat."

The food fueled Wight's growth, which never seemed to slow. When he was a junior at W.W. King, Wight was 6 feet, 9 inches and weighed 325 pounds—with 7 percent body fat.

He wore size-38 pants and a XXXXL shirt the day he walked into David Rankin's office and asked how a kid might sign up to play football.

"I said, 'What grade?' because I thought he had a young'un or something," Rankin says. "He said, 'I'm going to be a junior.'"

Football was Wight's first love, but basketball grabbed him by the ear and didn't let go. He was an unstoppable post presence, sure. But he liked to shoot 3-pointers. When the Knights had a lead that satisfied coach Bill Scyphers—70 points or so, Scyphers says—Wight had permission to leave the lane and pop 3-pointers until his shoulders ached.

He was an all-state player in 1990, his senior season, and had several scholarship offers to play college basketball. He spent a year at an Oklahoma junior college before playing the 1991–92 season at Wichita State.

Surgery and Its Aftermath

Wight was a 19-year-old sophomore when he noticed blurry spots in his vision. Regular checkups found nothing unusual, but his vision remained unclear. A trip to the Mayo Clinic, a renowned hospital in Minnesota, yielded an answer. There was a tumor on his pituitary gland, doctors said. It was smaller than a grain of sand. If it was not removed, Wight's vision might never improve. And he might never stop growing.

Surgery eliminated the tumor, but it came during the most difficult time in Wight's life. He gained about 100 pounds after the procedure, making basketball more difficult than ever. At the end of Wight's sophomore season, Wichita State coach Mike Cohen was fired. Soon afterward, Wight's father died of cancer.

Wight was finished with school. In the summer of 1992, he dropped out of Wichita State and shuffled among a handful of low-wage jobs. Wight's luck changed in 1994 when he was invited to appear in a celebrity basketball game in Illinois. One of his teammates was legendary wrestler Hulk Hogan, who was stunned by Wight's agility and size and offered to connect him with the right people in wrestling.

Wight, a longtime wrestling fan, accepted Hogan's invitation and began training.

In his first match, with World Championship Wrestling in 1995, Wight—known as "The Giant"—beat Hogan to win the world heavyweight championship.

Success—with a Price

Wight's wrestling success earned him a 10-year contract with WWE in 1999. It paid him about $1 million per year. His exposure also opened doors for movie roles and appearances in TV commercials.

He is a real-life giant, and he is more marketable when he is at his largest. His listed weight of 507 pounds is part of the show; to make the figure believable, Wight has weighed around 450 pounds since his 1995 debut.

But the heavier Wight is, the more his body breaks down. The weight strains his muscles and joints; he has had several knee surgeries, one of which deflated his chances of reviving his basketball career at a small college in Illinois. His mother says Wight has an enlarged heart, which she downplays as being part of the large package.

Still, the show must go on. And if Wight wants to be paid, he must weigh enough to look like a giant—and he must be silent about his weaknesses....

It was in late 2006, however, when Wight's body began breaking down to a point WWE could no longer hide it.

The Upside of Losing

It is all staged, of course. Scripted, yes. But ask any wrestler: It is sure not fake. The action, like a compelling tall tale, has a beginning, middle and end. The chaos is kept in order by, of all people, the referee. The wrestlers are the players. The referee is the director.

It is a Sunday night in December. This night's main event is billed as an "Extreme Elimination Chamber" match. Two wrestlers begin the match in the ring, and, according to the rules, four others will enter at random. A wrestler is eliminated by being pinned or disqualified. The last man standing among the six will be the Extreme Championship Wrestling heavyweight champion. ECW is a branch promotion of WWE.

The Big Show is the last wrestler to enter. All but Bobby Lashley, a chiseled man and a former college wrestler, have been eliminated. Neither of these facts happened by accident. Like the match's ending—Lashley pinned the Big Show to win the championship—Wight's entrance order and participation were scripted.

He spends 3 minutes, 42 seconds in the ring. The next-shortest appearance is more than twice that amount of time. Wight's movements, on offense and defense, are slow and careful. Wight, who once could execute a back flip off the top turnbuckle, now has trouble walking. At this stage of Wight's career, priority is placed on getting him in and out of the ring as quickly as possible.

He entered this night with a torn abdominal muscle, a bulging disk in his back, a weak ankle, a sprained wrist and a history of knee surgeries.

The injuries, and [the fact] that Wight's WWE contract will expire in three months, played into promoters' decision to relieve the Big Show of his championship. Wight accepted the decision with little commotion. After all, losing the title has an upside. His time out of the main-event spotlight means he can spend much of the final months of his contract doing what he could not for the past 10 years: healing.

It was his schedule—Wight's WWE contract, which expired in March [2007], required him to work 285 dates per year, not including travel days—that left few options for his at-home routine. Upon returning to Tampa, Wight visits a chiropractor. The next stop is the acupuncturist. His final destination, for as long as the calendar will allow, is his sofa.

Wight's mother, Dorothy, says her son has the body of a 70-year-old. That he smokes cigarettes and maintains a global travel schedule, Dorothy says, is reason to worry. And it is proof that her son's work is far from fake.

"The body is not designed for that," she says. "They (pro wrestlers) hurt. They bruise. They get beat up. They do stuff that sane people wouldn't do. It's time for him to give this up. He needs to give it up."

After the Final Bell

Three months after his WWE contract expired, Wight is gone. He is gone from wrestling. Gone from the United States and its demands. Reality, it would appear, can wait.

Dorothy Wight said her son and his wife, Bess, spent last month [May 2007] on vacation in Greece. It is Wight's chance to relax, unbutton his trousers and exhale.

For now, Wight can wrestle when he wants—and not one match more. A report on a pro wrestling Web site stated Wight wrestled Hulk Hogan, a longtime friend, last month in a small-promotion show in Memphis.

During a news conference before that match, Wight said he no longer would wrestle under the name "the Big Show," a moniker he jokingly referred to in April as his "slave name."

Wight said he was tired of living at the mercy of others, presumably promoters who profit from his obesity. It is a role he has played for more than a decade and one he played flawlessly. Wight sacrificed his body and his health in exchange for fame and fortune. It is a trade that eventually wore thin.

Dorothy Wight said Bess, who also works as Wight's manager, has invested much of the money Wight earned from his various occupations. Dorothy Wight said the couple would have no problem living comfortably, even if Wight never returns to wrestling.

Wight has lived 35 years as a giant, part of a tall tale. He might spend the next decade undoing the damage he did to his body during the past 13 years. Wight said during the Memphis news conference that he had lost 60 pounds since retiring after the December [2006] show in Augusta. He said he feels better, mentally and physically, than he has in more than a decade.

"Paul Wight, not the Big Show, is very intelligent," Dorothy Wight says. "Paul Wight is funny. He's articulate. He's a clown. He reads. He's Stephen King and *Star Trek*. Heavy stuff. When you get to know Paul the guy, he's a good, loyal friend."

Wight came to a crossroad that night in Augusta. There was something about the way he walked up the ramp after losing to Lashley. There was something about the way he paused and stared into the crowd. It was as if he was saying goodbye.

Less than 50 miles from his home, where the growth started and the wild stories of a giant man took flight, Wight turned and walked away. It was in Augusta that Paul Wight took the first steps out of the Big Show's skin.

Perhaps Wight realized tall tales are better without a sad ending.

> **FAST FACT**
>
> According to the Hormone Foundation, childhood gigantism is extremely rare, occurring in less than one hundred children in the United States.

GLOSSARY

achondroplasia   The most common form of dwarfism, in which the arms and legs of the person are very short, while the torso is of regular size.

acromegaly   A disease caused by the overproduction of growth hormone in the body.

adrenal glands   A pair of endocrine glands seated atop the kidneys that produce vital hormones.

apnea   A condition in which breathing slows or stops for short periods of time, often during sleep.

benign   Opposite of malignant; that is, not cancerous.

calcification   The strengthening of a bone in areas where calcium has been deposited.

cartilage   A dense elastic tissue that forms most of the skeleton in the human fetus but that is gradually replaced by bone during normal development.

congenital   Present from birth but not necessarily genetic. A congenital condition can be caused by a genetic mutation, an unfavorable environment in the uterus, or a combination of both factors.

connective tissue   The "glue" and scaffolding of the body that includes the substance between cells (extracellular matrix) consisting of collagen and elastic fibers.

cortisol   A hormone produced by the adrenal glands affecting fat storage, glucose production, and bone strength. It also helps the body handle the stress of illness or injury.

dwarfism   A family of growth disorders that result primarily from impaired development of bone and cartilage. Also known as disproportionate

Glossary

	short stature, which may manifest as short-limbed dwarfism or short-trunk dwarfism.
dysplasia	Abnormal development.
echocardiogram	A test that uses high-frequency sound waves to examine and take pictures of the heart and surrounding tissues.
endocrine glands	Organs of the body that produce and release hormones directly into the bloodstream.
genome	All the DNA contained in an organism or a cell, which includes both the chromosomes within the nucleus and the DNA in the mitochondria.
genotype	The genetic identity of an individual that does not show as outward characteristics.
gigantism	The term for acromegaly when it develops before the onset of puberty.
growth hormone	A hormone secreted by the pituitary gland. It regulates the production of protein for new cell development and stimulates bone growth in the growth plates at the end of bones.
growth hormone deficiency	A noticeable slowing of growth during infancy or childhood due to a lack of human growth hormone, resulting in abnormally short stature but with proportional limbs and trunk.
growth plate	A cartilage plate at the ends of the long bones of children where the lengthening of bone takes place.
heritable	Capable of being transmitted from parent to child.
hormone	A chemical "messenger" produced by an endocrine gland that targets various parts of the body, modifying its structure or changing its activity.
hypothalamus	A thumbnail-size part of the brain located just above the pituitary gland.
inherited	Transmitted through genes from parents to offspring.

Growth Disorders

malignant	Abnormal tissue growth that is locally invasive and capable of spreading; cancerous.
Marfan syndrome	A growth disorder caused by a mutation in the gene that produces the protein fillibrin. It causes an overgrowth and weakness of connective tissue, which can result in unusually long limbs, visual problems, and cardiac abnormalities.
mutation	Any alteration in a gene from its natural state, caused by a change in a DNA sequence.
nutritional short stature	Growth failure due to malnutrition, usually a lack of protein.
ossification	The process of bone formation.
phenotype	The observable traits or characteristics of an organism, such as hair color or the presence or absence of a disease.
pituitary gland	The small oval endocrine gland attached to the brain just behind the middle of the eyebrows that produces growth hormone.
sex chromosome	One of two chromosomes that specify an organism's genetic sex. Humans have two kinds of sex chromosomes, called X and Y; females have two X chromosomes, and males have one X and one Y.
Turner syndrome	A growth disorder in girls in which one X chromosome is missing. The disorder causes short stature, webbed neck, and premature ovarian failure, which leads to incomplete puberty.

CHRONOLOGY

1305   Vladislas Cubitas, a dwarf, becomes king of Poland.

1542   Mary, Queen of Scots, believed to have had Marfan syndrome, rules Scotland from 1542 until 1567.

1815   Primordial dwarfism is first identified in Caroline Cratchami, a girl born in Palermo, Italy. Appearing in exhibitions in London, she became known as the "Sicilian Fairy."

1840–1940   Traveling "freak shows," circuses, and carnivals often featuring people with growth disorders and other genetic abnormalities, are a prominent form of public entertainment.

1843   Charles Stratton, a dwarf known as "General Tom Thumb," is first exhibited by circus pioneer P.T. Barnum.

1860   Abraham Lincoln, believed to have had Marfan syndrome, becomes president of the United States.

1864   Henri Toulouse-Lautrec, the French postimpressionist painter, is born with a rare genetic growth disorder, pycnodysostosis, characterized by abnormal density of the bones.

1886   The term *acromegaly*, a form of gigantism, is first used by French neurologist Pierre Marie to describe a condition characterized by enlargement of the hands, feet, and face.

1896   French physician Antoine Marfan first recognizes the condition now called Marfan syndrome, a disorder related to the overgrowth and malfunctioning of the body's connective tissues.

1938   Oklahoma physician Henry Turner first describes the growth disorder specific to females that becomes known as Turner syndrome.

Growth Disorders

1939	One hundred and twenty-two adults with different forms of dwarfism, along with a dozen child actors, portray Munchkins in the movie *The Wizard of Oz*.
1951	Russian surgeon Gavriil A. Ilizarov begins developing the practice of limb-lengthening surgery after discovering that the external fixation frame he was using to treat bone fractures could stimulate new bone growth.
1956	Biochemist Choh Hao Li isolates human growth hormone from the pituitary gland.
1957	Dwarf Hollywood actor Billy Barty founds the Little People of America, an advocacy group for people with dwarfism.
1958	Human growth hormone is first used by Tufts University endocrinologist Maurice Raben to treat a seventeen-year-old male with growth hormone deficiency.
1959	Scientists identify the chromosomal basis of Turner syndrome.
1965	Cardiologist and medical geneticist Victor McKusick, who researched Marfan syndrome, dwarfism, and other genetic disorders, suggests that dwarfism is an umbrella term for many unique kinds of conditions.
1971	Biochemist Choh Hao Li and his associates produce the first synthetic form of human growth hormone.
1981	The National Marfan Foundation is established.
1984	Scientists discover that dwarfism is caused by a genetic mutation. The US Food and Drug Administration (FDA) approves biosynthetic growth hormone for use in children with growth hormone deficiency.
1985	The first four cases of individuals developing Creutzfeldt-Jakob disease after being injected with pituitary-derived growth hormone are discovered; thereafter, only biosynthetic, or recombinant human growth hormone (also known as somatropin or hGH), is used to treat certain growth disorders. Pediatric orthopedic surgeon James Aronson is the first to perform a leg-lengthening procedure in North America, using the Ilizarov technique.

Chronology

1986	The FDA approves the use of human growth hormone to enhance stature in Turner syndrome patients. US Olympic volleyball star Flo Hyman dies from an ruptured aorta, a frequent consequence of Marfan syndrome, while playing a match in Japan.
1987	The Turner Syndrome Society of the United States is founded.
1994	The gene for the most common form of dwarfism, achondroplasia, is identified.
1996	The FDA approves the used of hGH therapy for adults suffering from growth hormone deficiency as a result of other recognized medical conditions.
2002	Little People of America releases a statement advising people with dwarfism to avoid limb-lengthening surgery.
2009	The *Guinness Book of World Records* announces that Sultan Kosen of Turkey is the tallest man in the world. His eight feet once inch stature is the result of a pituitary tumor.
2011	A research team led by Ecuadoran endocrinologist Jaime Guevara-Aguirre discovers that a rare form of dwarfism may provide protection against cancer and diabetes.

ORGANIZATIONS TO CONTACT

The editors have compiled the following list of organizations concerned with the issues debated in this book. The descriptions are derived from materials provided by the organizations. All have publications or information available for interested readers. The list was compiled on the date of publication of the present volume; the information provided here may change. Be aware that many organizations take several weeks or longer to respond to inquiries, so allow as much time as possible.

American Heart Association
7272 Greenville Ave., Dallas, TX 75231
(800) 242-8721 (toll-free)
fax: (800) 474-8483 (toll-free)
website: www.heart.org

The American Heart Association is a national voluntary health agency to help reduce disability and death from cardiovascular illnesses. Its website provides information for patients, caregivers, consumers, and health care professionals as part of its goal to build healthier lives that are free of cardiovascular diseases and stroke. The home page features a search engine that links to information on the heart abnormalities frequently seen in patients with Marfan syndrome.

The Hormone Foundation
8401 Connecticut Ave., Ste. 900, Chevy Chase, MD 20815-5817
(800) 467-6663 (toll-free)
fax: (301) 941-0259
website: www.hormone.org

As the public education affiliate of the Endocrine Society, the Hormone Foundation provides hormone-related health information to patients, physicians, health professionals, and the media. The foundation offers free informational materials, a physician referral service, and media education campaigns as part of its mission to promote the prevention, treatment, and cure of endocrine disorders and hormone-related conditions. Its website includes a library of materials covering a wide range of hormone-related topics, including acromegaly, precocious puberty, growth disorders, and Turner syndrome.

Organizations to Contact

Human Growth Foundation
997 Glen Cove Ave., Ste. 5, Glen Head, NY 11545
(800) 451-6434 (toll-free)
fax: (516) 671-4055
website: www.hgfound.org

The Human Growth Foundation is a nonprofit volunteer organization whose goal is to provide relevant research, advocacy, support, and educational resources to people with growth disorders, metabolic diseases, and other hormone-related conditions. Its website, updated monthly, includes links to the reports "Disorders of Short Stature," and "Pediatric Growth Hormone Deficiency," as well as highlights of and invitations to participate in clinical trials and studies, including "Turner Syndrome Study (For 16–24-Year-Old Women with Turner Syndrome): Early Brain Development."

Little People of America (LPA)
250 El Camino Real, Ste. 201, Tustin, CA 92780
(714) 368-3689; toll-free: (888) 572-2001
fax: (714) 368-3367
e-mail: info@lpaonline.org
website: www.lpaonline.org

LPA is a national nonprofit organization that provides support and information to people of short stature and their families. LPA is the only dwarfism-support organization that includes all those with any of the more than two hundred medical conditions referred to as dwarfism. LPA offers information on education, employment, disability rights, adoption, medical issues, adaptive issues, and parenting children with dwarfism. The organization also publishes a national newsletter, *LPA Today*, and its website provides links to reports, articles, frequently asked questions, discussion groups, and other agencies that support little people, such as the Dwarf Athletic Association of America.

MAGIC Foundation
6645 W. North Ave., Oak Park, IL 60302
(708) 383-0808; toll-free: (800) 362-4423
fax: (708) 383-0899
website: www.magicfoundation.org

Major Aspects of Growth in Children (MAGIC) is made up of more than twenty-five thousand families whose children (and affected adults) have growth hormone deficiency or other medical conditions that interfere with normal growth. The foundation is devoted to disseminating information and sharing resources about the variety of factors that can affect growth; in particular it wishes to provide support for parents who are searching for answers about their children who have yet to be diagnosed with a specific growth disorder. Its website features a searchable database on various topics, including growth hormone deficiency, idiopathic short stature, precocious puberty, and Turner syndrome.

Growth Disorders

March of Dimes Foundation
1275 Mamaroneck Ave., White Plains, NY 10605
(914) 997-4488
website: www.marchofdimes.com

The March of Dimes Foundation is a nonprofit organization whose goal is to improve the health of babies by preventing birth defects, premature birth, and infant mortality. It was founded in 1938 by US president Franklin D. Roosevelt as a charitable foundation to defeat polio, which was one of the most devastating childhood illnesses in the mid-twentieth century. Currently, the March of Dimes funds research in biochemistry, developmental biology, genetics, pediatrics, and many other fields related to infant health. Articles and reports on chromosomal abnormalities, achondroplasia, Marfan syndrome, and other growth disorders are available on its website.

National Endocrine and Metabolic Diseases Information Service
6 Information Way, Bethesda, MD 20892-3569
(888) 828-0904 (toll-free)
fax: (703) 738-4929
website: http://endocrine.niddk.nih.gov/

This US governmental organization is an information dissemination service of the National Institute of Diabetes and Digestive and Kidney Diseases (NIDDK), a member of the National Institutes of Health. The NIDDK conducts and supports biomedical research, and as a public service it has established various information outlets to increase knowledge and understanding about health and disease among patients, health professionals, and US communities. The online database available at the website of the National Endocrine and Metabolic Disease Information Service provides links to reports, studies, and medical journal articles about Turner syndrome and issues affecting people treated with human growth hormone.

National Institute of Child Health and Human Development (NICHD)
31 Center Dr., Bldg. 31, Rm. 2A32, MSC 2425
Bethesda, MD 20892-2425
(800) 370-2943 (toll-free)
fax: (866) 760-5947 (toll-free)
website: www.nichd.nih.gov

The NICHD was initially established to investigate the broad aspects of human development as a means of understanding developmental disorders and disabilities and how they are related to events that occur during pregnancy. Currently, the institute conducts and supports research on all stages of human development, from preconception to adulthood, to better understand the health of children, adults, families, and communities. Its website features an A-to-Z library of fact sheets about various growth disorders, including Turner syndrome, precocious puberty, and pituitary tumors.

Organizations to Contact

National Marfan Foundation (NMF)
22 Manhasset Ave., Port Washington, NY 11050
(516) 883-8712; toll-free: (800) 862-7326
fax: (516) 883-8040
website: www.marfan.org

NMF, founded in 1981, is a nonprofit voluntary health organization with the goal of saving lives and improving the quality of life for individuals and families affected by Marfan syndrome and related disorders. NMF promotes research to improve diagnosis and treatment, advocates for federal funding, provides educational resources, and offers support services for people living with Marfan syndrome. Its website provides detailed information on the cause, characteristics, effects, and treatments for the disorder and features a "Teen Space" page with links to social advice written by youths with Marfan syndrome.

National Organization for Rare Disorders (NORD)
PO Box 8923, New Fairfield, CT 06812-8923
(203) 746-6518
website: www.rarediseases.org

Founded in 1983, NORD is a nongovernmental federation of voluntary health agencies aiming to help people who have rare "orphan" diseases (disorders that affect fewer than two hundred thousand people in the United States), and assisting the organizations that serve them. NORD is committed to the identification, treatment, and cure of rare disorders through programs of education, advocacy, research, and service. As a clearinghouse for information on rare disorders, its website provides a database of reports on more than twelve hundred conditions, including acromegaly, achondroplasia and other forms of dwarfism, Marfan syndrome, Turner syndrome, and other growth disorders.

The Nemours Center for Children's Health Media and Kidshealth.org
1600 Rockland Rd., Wilmington, DE 19803
(302) 651-4075
fax: (302) 651-4077
website: www.kidshealth.org

Established in 1936 by Alfred L. Dupont, Nemours is a nonprofit organization dedicated to improving children's health. Nemours supports clinical research that transforms scientific advances into practical ways to improve health care for young people, and through its various advocacy and prevention programs, it develops ways to work with communities to help children grow up healthy. The Nemours Center for Children's Health Media creates the website Kidshealth.org as well as other online, print, and video resources that provide health education for families and teachers. Fact sheets and articles at Kidshealth.org include information on growth disorders, precocious puberty, and endocrinology.

Growth Disorders

Pituitary Network Association (PNA)
PO Box 1958, Thousand Oaks, CA 91358
(800) 499-9973 (toll-free)
fax: (805) 480-0633
e-mail: info@pituitary.org
website: www.pituitary.org

The PNA is an international nonprofit organization for patients with pituitary tumors and diseases and for their families, caregivers, and health care providers. Founded in 1992 by a group of acromegalic patients in order to communicate their experiences and concerns, PNA has become the world's largest advocacy organization devoted to the treatment and cure of pituitary disorders. Supported by an international network of physicians and surgeons, the goal of the PNA is to create public awareness programs, provide educational resources, and assist the medical community in diagnosing, treating, and curing pituitary disorders. Its interactive website includes the article "Introduction to the Pituitary Gland" as well as fact sheets on pituitary tumors, growth hormone deficiency, and other neuroendocrine disorders.

Turner Syndrome Society of the United States (TSSUS)
11250 West Rd., Ste. G, Houston, TX 77065
(800) 365-9944 (toll-free)
fax: (832) 912-6446
website: www.turnersyndrome.org

The TSSUS is a nonprofit organization that provides health-related resources to patients, families, and physicians for the diagnosis and treatment of Turner syndrome. The society was originally created in 1987 by a group of women in Chicago, Illinois, for the purpose of networking and support. Today the organization holds an annual conference featuring medical experts, social workers, educators, and psychologists, providing opportunities for information exchange among Turner patients, care providers, and families. The TSSUS website offers access to the handbooks *Turner Syndrome: A Guide for Families*, and *A Guide for Girls with TS*, as well as links to press releases and research studies.

FOR FURTHER READING

Books

Betty M. Adelson, *Dwarfism: Medical and Psychosocial Aspects of Profound Short Stature*. Baltimore: Johns Hopkins University Press, 2005.

Robert Cabitt, *The Case of the Telltale Toes: Marfan Syndrome — Sinister Genetic Disorder of Seven Look-Alike Celebrities*. Broomfield, CO: FeedBrewer, 2011.

Lisa Graff, *The Thing About Georgie*. New York: HarperCollins, 2008.

Shirley Hiter, *Big Things in Little Packages: My Growing Up with Turner Syndrome*. Raleigh, NC: Lulu.com, 2010.

Victoria Hockfield, *Dwarfism and Gigantism: Causes, Treatment, and List of Shortest and Tallest People in the World*. Billings, MT: Hockfield, 2010.

Paul Kaplowitz, *Early Puberty in Girls: The Essential Guide to Coping with this Common Problem*. New York: Ballantine, 2004.

Paul Kaplowitz and Jeffrey Bacon, *The Short Child: A Parent's Guide to the Causes, Consequences, and Treatment of Growth Problems*. New York: Wellness Central, 2006.

Dan Kennedy, *Little People: Learning to See the World Through My Daughter's Eyes*. Emmaus, PA: Rodale, 2003.

Robert Marion, *Genetic Rounds: A Doctor's Encounters in the Field That Revolutionized Medicine*. Washington, DC: Kaplan, 2010.

Philip M. Parker, *Marfan Syndrome: A Bibliography and Dictionary for Physicians, Patients, and Genome Researchers*. San Diego: Icon Group International, 2007.

Jennifer Phillips, *Robert Wadlow: The Unique Life of the Boy Who Became the World's Tallest Man.* Charleston, SC: CreateSpace, 2010.

John Schwartz, *Short: Walking Tall When You're Not Tall at All.* New York: Flash Point, 2010.

Ashley Whitaker, *A Young Woman's Journey with Asperger's and Turner Syndrome.* Bloomington, IN: Xlibris, 2009.

Periodicals and Internet Sources

Gaill Appleson, "Washington U. Targets Genetic Disorder Among Tall People," *St. Louis Post-Dispatch*, September 17, 2009.

Elvira Cordileone, "Small in Stature but Big in Heart: Teenager Overcomes Disorder That Stunts Her Growth," *Toronto Star*, March 20, 2008.

Caitlin Gibson, "For Caitlin Schroeder, Achieving Near-Average Height Would Require No Small Act of Courage," *Washington Post Magazine*, November 30, 2008.

Health and Medicine Week, "RNA Interference Therapy Heals Growth Deficiency Disorder in a Live Animal," December 31, 2007.

Mark Henderson, "Hope for Women Whose Babies Stop Growing in Womb," *Times* (London), April 14, 2009.

Jim Leavesley, "Honest Abe's Curse," *Australian Doctor*, November 28, 2008.

S. Melmed, "Medical Progress: Acromegaly," *New England Journal of Medicine*, December 14, 2006.

Gretchen Parker, "Limb Lengthening Tests Human Willpower," MSNBC, February 18, 2004. www.msnbc.com.

Robyn Passante, "Family Struggles to Battle Child's Growth Disorder," *Hilton Head (SC) Island Packet*, August 24, 2008.

Roni Rabin, "It Seems the Fertility Clock Clicks for Men, Too," *New York Times*, February 27, 2007.

Wendy Ruderman, "Life Defines Her Stature," *Philadelphia Inquirer*, August 26, 2006.

Lisa Sanders, "Sleepless," *New York Times Magazine*, May 10, 2009.

States News Service, "New Diagnostic Criteria for Marfan Syndrome," July 2, 2010.

Nikhil Swaminathan, "What Causes Gigantism?," *Scientific American*, August 14, 2008.

INDEX

A

Achondroplasia (short-limb dwarfism)
 cause of, 28–29, 112–113, 114–115
 prevalence of, 28, 114
 prognosis of, 32
 symptoms of, 31–32, *103*, *113*
 x-ray of skull in, *41*
 x-ray of torso in, *29*
Acromegaly, 13–14
 cause of, 25, 35–36
 diagnosis of, 39–40
 symptoms of, 34–35
 treatment of, 40–44
ACTH, 75, 76
Actors, 100–101
Adelson, Betty M., 94, 97, 98
Adenomas, 36, 38
ADHD (attention deficit hyperactivity disorder), 122
Adrenal crisis, 74–79
Adrenal glands, 26
 function of, 75
 hormones produced by, 76
Aging, 13
Ain, Michael, 104–105
Alternative Medicine (journal), 82, 83
American Recovery and Reinvestment Act (2009), 114
Aneurysms, 49
Arnold, Gary, 97, 99, 126
Attention deficit hyperactivity disorder (ADHD), 122

B

Baker, Kenny, 101
Barty, Billy, 30–31, 97, 98, 101
Barzilai, Nir, 12–13
Beta blockers, 50, 55
Biro, Frank M., 87
Blood tests, 39
Bone, *20*
Bone disorders, 21
Breast cancer, 87–88
Brody, Jane E., 68

C

Cancer, 14
 IGF-1 and, 73
 Laron syndrome and, 12–13
 precocious puberty and, 87–88
Celebrity Apprentice (TV program), 93, 127
Celiac disease, 57
Children/adolescents, stature for age in, *23*
Chondrodystrophy, 45
Chromosome(s)

associated with Marfan syndrome, 53
karyotype in Turner syndrome, *60*
in Turner syndrome, *132*
Chronic diseases, 21
CJD (Creutzfeldt-Jakob disease), 66, 75
Colburn, Theo, 82
Collette, 131
Computerized tomography (CT) scan, 40, 49
Cortisol, 26, 74, 76
  adrenal crisis and, 79
Creutzfeldt-Jakob disease (CJD), 66, 75
CT (computerized tomography) scan, 40, 49
Cushing's syndrome, 26

D
Department of Health and Human Services, US (DHHS), 65
Dinklage, Peter, 94–95
Dolgoff, Joanna, 86
Dopamine agonists, 43
Dowshen, Steven A., 16
Dozier, Cutler, 70–71
Dumanoski, Diane, 82
Dwarf, as term, 98
Dwarfism, 10
  acceptance of, 102–106
  appropriate terms for sufferers of, 96–97
  prevention of, 112–117
  recognition of cause of, 10–11
  symptoms of, *103*

See also Achondroplasia
Dysplasia, 45

E
Ear infections, in Turner syndrome, 61
Echocardiogram, 49, 50, 55, 60
Electrocardiogram (EKG), 49
Endocrine disruptors, 81, 82–83
Endocrine glands, *78*
Endocrinologists, *70*
Exercise, 52–53
Extended limb-lengthening (ELL). *See* Limb-lengthening surgery

F
Failure to thrive (FTT), 22
FGFR3 gene, 28–29, 114
Fibrillin genes, 53
Food and Drug Administration, US (FDA), 64, 66
Freak shows, 11–12
Frey, Rebecca J., 27

G
GH. *See* Growth hormone
GH receptor antagonists (GHRAs), 42–43
GHRH (growth hormone-releasing hormone), 36, 39
Gigantism, 10
  cause of, 25
  excessive growth hormone leads to, 33–44
See also Acromegaly
Gordon, Philippa, 69

Growth Disorders

Graff, Lisa, 102, 103
Greene, Alan, 83
Growth
  abnormal, 21–22
  defining normal, 17–18
  during puberty, 18
  of long bones, 20
  mechanism of, 20–21
Growth disorder(s)
  personal account of pro wrestler with, 135–143
  prevalence of, 10
Growth hormone (GH), 129
  first isolation of, 10
  injections, 68–73
  levels in acromegaly, 37
  measurement of, 39–40
  recipients may be at risk for adrenal crisis, 74–79
  role of, 63
  in treatment of achondroplasia, 32
  use/abuse of, 62–66
Growth hormone deficiency
  hGH injections benefit people with, 68–73
  personal account of boy suffering, 128–130
Growth hormone-releasing hormone (GHRH), 36, 39
Guevara-Aguirre, Jaime, 12

H
Hankins, Sheryl, 99
Harris, Lynn, 92
Health risks
  of early puberty, 87–89
  of extended limb-lengthening, 109
Heart abnormalities
  in Marfan syndrome, 47, 50–51
  in Turner syndrome, 60–61
Heavin, Janese, 125
Height
  for age in children/adolescents, 23
  variations in, 17–18
  in women with/without Turner syndrome, 58
Herman-Giddens, Marcia, 81, 83
hGH (human growth hormone). See Growth hormone
Hoernschemeyer, Dan, 126
Hogan, Hulk, 140
The Hormone Foundation, 62
Hormones, 22, 23
Hristova, Kalina, 113, 114, 116–117
Human growth hormone (hGH). See Growth hormone
Hunter, Lucy, 119
Hyperpituitarism, 25
Hyperthyroidism, 26
Hypochondroplasia, 103
Hypopituitarism, 24
Hypothalamus, 18–19, 36
Hypothyroidism, 25–26
  in Turner syndrome, 61

I
Insulin-like growth factor I (IGF-I), 36, 44, 73
Intrauterine growth retardation (IUGR), 21

Index

Izenberg, Neil, 16

J
Johns Hopkins University Office of News and Information, 112

K
Kaplowitz, Paul, 83
Karyotype, 57
  in Turner syndrome, *60*
Kennedy, Dan, 102
Kidney problems, 61
Korpai, Darlene, 93–94
Korpai, Hailey, 93–94
Korpai, Jimmy, 93–94

L
Laron syndrome, 12–13
Limb-lengthening surgery/procedures (ELL), *108*
  acceptance of dwarfism is preferable to, 102–106
  implant used in, *105*
  numerous complications of, 107–111
Lincoln, Abraham, 22
Little people
  are demeaned in popular culture, 92–101
  seek tolerance, 125–127
  as term, 31, 98
Little People of America (LPA), 30–31, 92, 101, 106
Little People of America Medical Advisory Board, 107
Longo, Valter, 13

Lung problems, 48

M
MAGIC Foundation, 133
Magnetic resonance imaging (MRI), 40, 49, 60
March of Dimes Foundation, 45
Marfan, Antoine, 46
Marfan syndrome, 10, 22
  cause of, 53–54
  diagnosis of, 49–50
  effects of, 46–49, 120
  famous people/historical figures with, 54, 123
  feet in, *121*
  issues related to, 52–53
  personal account of affected mother, 119–124
  pregnancy and, 54–55
  prevalence of, 46
  symptoms of, *48*
  treatment of, 50–53
  x-ray of hands in, *46*
McGimsey, Mark, 125–126, 127
Media, dwarfism in, 103–105
Merck Manual of Medical Information, 38
Midget, as offensive term, 96–98
MRI (magnetic resonance imaging), 40, 49, 60
Mueller, Gillian, 104
Myers, John Peterson, 82

N
National Endocrine and Metabolic Diseases Information Service, 33, 74

National Youth Risk Behavior Survey, 90
New York Times (newspaper), 97
Nonpituitary tumors, 39
Nutrition, 21

O
Obesity
  early puberty is linked to, 86–91
  prevalence among boys, *88*
  prevalence among high school students, 90
Obstruction apnea, 31
Osteoarthritis, *110*
Osteoblasts, 21
Our Stolen Future (Colburn et al.), 82

P
Paley, Dror, 104, 105
PCOS (polycystic ovarian syndrome), 89
Pediatrics (journal), 70, 71, 81, 86
Peter the Great (Russian czar), 11
Pituitary gland, 22, 26
  light micrograph of tissue types in, *63*
  role in growth hormone production, 36
  tumors of, 36, 38
Polycystic ovarian syndrome (PCOS), 89
Polyvinyl chloride (PVC), 85
Povinelli, Mark, 99–100
Prader-Willi syndrome, 71
Precocious puberty, 18–19
  environmental toxins are linked to, 80–85
  is linked to obesity, 86–91
  prevalence of, 81
  symptoms of, *82*
Pregnancy, 54–55
Puberty
  delayed, 19–20
  growth during, 18
PVC (polyvinyl chloride), 85

R
Race/ethnicity, 89–90
Radiation therapy, 43–44
Ridley, Kim, 80
Ross, Judith L., 69, 71
Rubenstein, Zelda, 101
Ruppe, Mary, 10

S
Sanghavi, Darshak, 81
Schroeder, Caitlin, 104, 105
Sellman, Sherrill, 84–85
Short Persons Support, 111
Skeletal abnormalities, 47–48
Sneiderman, Phil, 112
Somatostatin, 36
Somatostatin analogs (SSAs), 42
Somatropin, 71
Spiegel, Barbara, 98
Spondyloepiphyseal dysplasia congenita, *103*
SSAs (somatostatin analogs), 42
The Station Agent (film), 94–95, 100
Steele, Michael, 126
Stereotactic radiation delivery, 43–44

Stramondo, Joe, 100
Stratton, Charles (Tom Thumb), 11, *11*
Surgery
  heart, 51
  in treatment of acromegaly, 41–42
  See also Limb-lengthening procedures

T
Testosterone, 81–82
The Thing About Georgie (Graff), 102–103
Thumb, Tom (Charles Stratton), 11
Thyroid, 22, 25–26
Thyroxine, 26
Treatment(s)
  achondroplasia, 31–32
  acromegaly, 40–44
  adrenal crisis, 77, 79
  Marfan syndrome, 50
  precocious puberty, 19
  See also Limb-lengthening surgery/procedures

Troyer, Verne, 101
TS. *See* Turner syndrome
TSSS (Turner Syndrome Support Society), 133
Turner, Henry, 57
Turner syndrome (TS), 10, 22
  average height in women with/without, *58*
  characteristics of, 57–58, *59*
  karyotype of chromosomes in, *60*
  personal account of impact of, 131–134
Turner Syndrome Society of the United States, 56
Turner Syndrome Support Society (TSSS), 133

V
Villachaize, Hervé, 101

W
Wight, Dorothy, 137, 138–139, 142, 143
Wight, Paul, *138*

BRADNER LIBRARY
SCHOOLCRAFT COLLEGE
LIVONIA, MICHIGAN 48152